The Lockbox

Steven J Taylor

This is a work of fiction. The names, characters, places and incidents are products of the author's imagination or are used fictitiously. Any resemblance to persons living or dead is entirely coincidental.

I dedicate this book to my loving wife Audrey. She has been my biggest supporter throughout this entire process and my daily inspiration.

Prologue

Secret operations are essential in war; upon them the army relies to make its every move.

-Sun Tzu

November 21st, 1963
Bend, Oregon

The sun rose on another late fall morning. Winter's cruel touch had made an early appearance while blanketing the world in an unforgiving, arctic embrace. Each gust from the frigid tempest punished bare skin and transposed the landscape with every flake of snow it shifted.

Through the veil of desolate cold, the small town of Bend was already beginning to stir after another night of peaceful slumber. The townsfolk had begun their daily routines, blissfully ignorant to the storm rising from within their borders.

Unbeknownst to the people of this small town, a silent danger had moved in. Strangers had been seen skulking about the streets at night. They were journeymen without a sense of purpose, but always searching for something.

The local authorities had heard stories, but the sheriff chalked them up to nothing more than just a few transients passing through. This town had seen its fair share of tough times in the past decade and poverty wasn't anything new to the area.

Even though the authorities had decided to look the other way, these drifters were being watched by someone. Every movement stalked by a master of deceit, the shadow of all shadows.

If you asked those who came in contact with him, his description was always vague, jumbled. Some thought his age varied from early twenties to late thirties. He had been six foot three, five foot two, and even a woman. The truth is that no one had been able to recall with any certainty what this "mystery man" looked like. Yes, Gerald Simmons was the best at what he did. In a short amount of time, he had become the most talented spy the United States government had ever produced.

It had been three years since Gerald entered the secretive world of the Central Intelligence Agency, and his natural abilities had made him an asset to this country. Being a slight man with no distinguishing features, Agent Simmons had quickly learned the necessary skills he would need to become the perfect reconnaissance tool.

The international landscape had changed after the end of World War II. No longer could you count on looking your adversaries in the eye. Wars were now fought behind desks, the orders being given by politicians and crooks.

This kind of warfare didn't need GI's, it needed average looking men and women who could listen, watch, and act without detection. A "ghost without a conscience" is how his superiors described the modern soldier of the Cold War, not quite the life he had envisioned when signing up for the Marines eight years prior.

At the ripe age of twenty-six, Gerald still craved recognition. He desperately wanted to be perceived as the dangerous, suave spy that every woman swooned over. Unfortunately he knew his place, and that lifestyle would have to remain a fantasy revisited each night in his dreams.

It had been a couple weeks since he was given the somewhat obscure assignment of shadowing Shawn Grieve, former Deputy Secretary of Defense, and they had been the longest two weeks of his young life. After spending two years working undercover in Moscow, Gerald was brought back to the States and given this task with very little information pertaining to his target. All he knew is that this man was of great interest to the Agency and that every one of his movements needed to be strictly observed, and promptly reported back to his superiors at Langley on a daily basis.

Frustration had set in almost immediately. Gerald was trained to follow some of the most dangerous men in the world, and now he was babysitting a senior citizen in the middle of nowhere.

Each day, Gerald had to stay attentive through the monotony of what was Shawn's life. Shawn was a solitary man who seldom ever associated with anyone. He was a large man in his mid-fifties; and the passing of time had not been kind to him.

His stringy, shoulder length hair had turned a blinding shade of silver. Under his bushy, salt-n-pepper beard, the lines that cut into his face carried a lifetime of stress and sorrow. He was the definition of a broken man, and Gerald pitied him at times.

The information Gerald was able to dig up on his target before the mission, did little to help him understand why Shawn was so important.

ς

Born November 24th, 1906 in Boulder, Colorado, Shawn had lived the American dream. He was an All-American football star who drew attention and admiration for his good looks and intelligence along with his athletic heroics.

After he graduated high school, Shawn tried his hands at many different careers. He was working as a masonry apprentice when the country was thrust into the Great Depression of 1929. After that it only took a few months for the work to dry up and he found himself on the streets. Having just married his high school sweetheart, Shawn was burdened with more responsibilities but no way to make a living.

It was just after the birth of his first child in 1931 that he enlisted in the U.S. Army to help support his family. Following basic training, Shawn was able to utilize his physical and intellectual gifts to help rise swiftly through the ranks.

Soon after he attained the rank of Captain, the Japanese launched their attack on Pearl Harbor and America was thrust into World War II.

As part of the 29th Infantry, Shawn was decorated for valor due to his bravery during the D-Day invasion. His platoon was in the initial wave that landed at Omaha Beach, and it was only because of his quick thinking and leadership that six of his fellow soldiers made it home.

Following the war, Shawn retired from the Army. After retiring, he still had the urge to give back to his country, and this led him into seeking a place in the state government. It started with a brief turn as the Colorado State Comptroller; from there it was a quick ascension for Shawn into the heart of the political world.

Shawn's first bid for office in his home state of Colorado was successful. The next step secured him a Senate seat, and from there he never looked back. After cutting his teeth in the Senate for over a decade, Shawn was asked to become the Deputy Secretary of Defense under Secretary Neil H. McElroy; he graciously accepted. He served diligently from 1957-1959, and then without warning, resigned his post.

There were always questions about why he left only a month before Secretary McElroy was to step down. The official explanation was illness due to stress. However, in reality the details of his disappearance remained a mystery to both his friends and family.

Shawn had returned home from work on the afternoon of June 3rd, packed a bag and just vanished. He left a wife, three children, a lucrative career, and all the power a man could desire, along with many questions that needed answering.

Over the years since he left, the government had spared no expense trying to locate him. The reasons for their unrelenting search were a mystery to Gerald, but every soldier learns early on to never question the men at the top.

There were many false sightings, but since he remained at large, Shawn appeared to be an elusive adversary. That was until six months ago when Shawn would be discovered out of sheer dumb luck. It was during the yearly carnival that he had made the mistake of allowing his photo to be taken by a local reporter for the town. A few weeks passed and the photo found its way to Washington, precipitating the government into sending their best man to gather whatever information he could about their mystery fugitive.

Unfortunately, the government was not the only party interested in locating Shawn. Shortly after Gerald had arrived in Bend, others began to appear. Some he didn't know, others he had seen before. Bend, Oregon had quietly become the spy capital of the world.

$$\mathcal{S}$$

Blissfully unaware of the increased flow of newcomers, Shawn continued his normal schedule and today had been as drab and uneventful as every other.

After Shawn finished his daily walk along the frozen Deschutes River, he visited Joe's Diner for a late, solitary lunch.

From there he made his way to the town library where he worked part-time under the alias Robert Klein. Following his return to Joe's for a small dinner, Shawn headed back to his secluded cabin on the outskirts of town.

Gerald followed him then parked just around the corner from the cabin. It was time to settle in for another lackluster evening.

With the temperature now dropping below twenty degrees most nights, Gerald would stay until the lights went out, then he would probably return to the dismal hotel room he had called "home" since arriving.

After doing the daily crossword puzzle, Gerald checked his watch. He had just a few more tedious hours to go, but little did he know that all hell was about to break loose.

ॐ

A steady snow had begun to fall, covering the streets in a blanket of fresh powder. In the distance a pair of yellow headlights broke through the darkness.

The curtain of snow helped disguise the vehicle until it had pulled up outside of Shawn's cabin. The large black Mercedes had extinguished its lights as it approached the softly lit structure, making sure that its final approach would go unnoticed.

Three men exited the vehicle, each one larger than the next. All three wore thick, black trench coats with black fedoras pulled down over their eyes. The oppressive darkness and blowing snow made it difficult for Gerald to pin-point any distinguishing features of the men; he could only make out the steam coming from their shadowy forms.

The strangers approached the cabin and began pounding fiercely on the front door. After a few minutes, the largest of the three lifted his gigantic foot and busted through the red oak door. Following a short, tense silence, the men dragged Shawn out by his hair and threw him into the snow.

Witnessing the ferocity of the beating the men had begun to inflict on Shawn, Gerald knew that he had to intervene, but to what extent was he was willing to get involved?

He could not afford to expose his cover, but if anything happened to Shawn, Gerald would never be able to live with himself. When the monsters increased the volatile cadence of their blows, he realized he needed to act.

After slowly exiting his vehicle, he crouched down next to the fender, waiting for the ideal moment to strike. With their backs turned to him, Gerald sprinted to the opposite side of the cabin and quietly made his way behind a stack of firewood adjacent to the brutal attack. Two of the men were continuously kicking Shawn, who now cowered in a fetal position on the ground. The third man was standing just out of harm's way, observing the beating with a sadistic grin and sense of amusement.

He barked orders to the two larger thugs and screamed at Shawn in a broken French accent, asking him where "it" was.

Gerald crept stealthily behind the large man. He knew that timing would be everything and set a game plan in his head. Erupting at his target, Gerald swiftly snapped the interrogators neck. Luckily, the other two men enjoyed kicking Shawn too much to notice the sudden silence.

Regrouping his strength, Gerald leapt from the limp body of the first man to his next target. With a quick jab of his knife, he was able to slice the man's throat, and turn in time to block the attack of the third and final assailant.

Shoving the man back, Gerald had created enough space between them to deliver a brutal roundhouse kick to his head, knocking him unconscious. Leaping atop the motionless assailant, Gerald buried his knife into the large man's chest with a brutality and precision that only the most intense military training could prepare you for.

Staggering back into the side of the snow covered cabin, Gerald rested a minute; trying his best to absorb the macabre scene that lay before him. Shock would lead to disappointment and anger over the rookie mistake he had just made.

His unbridled rage had left all the participants bleeding out into the softly falling snow. You will never get information from a dead man, and Gerald had many questions that needed answering.

Snapping out of his daze, Gerald quickly rushed to Shawn's side.

Lying on a bed of crimson snow, Shawn's face had been crushed with the blows delivered by the assailants' feet, his body bent and broken beyond recognition. Gerald fell to his knees and cradled his head. He did his best to comfort Shawn, realizing that his wounds were most likely fatal.

"Try not to move Mr. Grieve. I'm here to help." With the shock of the situation still overwhelming to him, Gerald remained calm and continued to console the dying man.

"I'll get you out of here, just hang on."

Shawn opened his swollen eyes, and addressed his savior.

"Please …," is the only word Shawn can muster, his jaw most certainly broken. Reaching out, he grabbed Gerald's arm in a feeble grip.

Trembling, Shawn reached into his jacket pocket. He pulled out an envelope covered in fresh blood from the fractured rib now protruding from his chest. Handing it to Gerald, Shawn is only able to utter two words,

"Keep … safe."

Gerald cautiously accepted the envelope just as Shawn took his last breath. Realizing that he was gone, Gerald lowered Shawn's head gently to the ground.

As he stood and placed the envelope into his jacket, he paused and looked around at the carnage, knowing that it would be hard to explain the events to the local authorities.

After one last remorseful glance at Shawn's lifeless body, Gerald vanished into the night; the fresh canopy of snow covering any sign that he was ever there.

Chapter

One

July 23rd, 2012

2:35pm

Shashone Peak, Wyoming

"Oh crap."

These are the famous last words spoken by millions of children throughout the years; it's the phrase uttered upon realizing that once their parents have found out what they did, their lives might just be over.

Samuel Lana stood over a sea of broken glass. He ran his fingers through his shaggy blonde hair and cursed under his breath. At six-three and one hundred ninety five pounds, this sixteen year old was an easy target when blame was being passed around. Every time he got angry, things around him had the tendency to go boom.

He kicked the remains of the bay window that used to accent the lovely sitting room in which he stood; the same room his parents had spent the last two years decorating with antiques from around the world. Glass shards now littered the beautiful oak flooring which had been polished to a brilliant shine only three days prior.

After briefly pondering the mess he was in, Sam turned and looked down the hall at his accomplice, his sister Emily. "Now you did it, dumbass!"

"Don't you dare try pinning this on me," Emily shouted back as she entered the room. She was grinning from ear-to-ear as she walked over to Sam.

Though she was a year younger and half his size, Emily was notoriously apt at weaseling her way out of trouble that she usually caused. "If it wasn't for you being a jerk, I wouldn't have thrown that mug at your stupid head in the first place."

"Well maybe if you kept your nose out of my damn business, I wouldn't have to tweet pictures of you on the toilet." Sam pushed his sister, easily sending her much smaller frame crashing into the arm of the couch and off onto a side table.

Emily quickly recovered and sprang to her feet like a well-trained ninja. Her jet black hair slashed through the air as she swung her leg into Sam's torso, knocking him back onto the couch.

Leaping on top of him, she began beating his head with her fists. In self-defense, Sam instinctively smacked her in the nose with the palm of his hand. Emily's head whipped back as she screamed in agony, blood spraying all over the couch.

Responding to the crash and subsequent arguing of her children, Meghan Lana raced towards the room. Being a petite woman in her late thirties, Meghan is not what you would call an intimidating figure, but when she is pushed, watch out.

"What the hell is going on in there", she howled.

As Meghan turned the corner into her precious sitting room, she was shocked to see the empty frame where the shattered window once sat. Scanning the room, she focused on the two children who she once loved, wrestling on her two thousand dollar white leather couch, now littered with glass and blood.

Realizing that their mother had entered the room, Emily and Sam stopped dead in their tracks and slowly looked into the face of their own reckoning. Backing away from each other, the kids bowed their heads and braced for the inevitable storm.

Meghan took a moment to absorb all that she has just witnessed. She studied the empty pane followed by the glorious couch in which she found peace in her daily naps, and finally her antique end table from Egypt which used to have four legs; then she looked at her children with a burning feeling of rage mixed with crushing disappointment. The veins in her neck had begun pulsating to the point that it appeared her head might explode.

Taking a deep breath, Meghan tried to wipe the tears from the corner of her eyes, her hands trembling uncontrollably.

"I don't want any excuses from either of you," she patiently instructed the culprits, trying desperately to remain calm," I just want this mess cleaned up, NOW!" Punctuating her last word to get the desired result, Meghan turned and left the room, the shock still overwhelming.

Knowing that the fallout from this incident was far from over, Emily and Sam began to clean their mess, both kids glaring at each other as they worked.

ဢ

4:30pm

Thomas Jefferson High School

Rodger Lana enjoyed this time of day more than any other. He had spent the last six hours working with the coaching staff and his players to hopefully build the next great powerhouse in high school football, but now he was alone on the field, left with his thoughts.

For the last fifteen years, he had been a teacher and coach at Jefferson High. After growing up in New York City for the first eighteen years of his life, this small town in rural Wyoming had become his Eden.

Following his graduation from high school, he was accepted to Westminster College in Salt Lake City, Utah. After five long years of study, he would receive his Master's Degree in Education; but more importantly, it was over this time that he would meet his beautiful wife and soul mate, Meghan.

Three months before they both graduated from college, the unexpected happened when Meghan became pregnant with their first child. After graduation, the young couple made the choice to move back to Meghan's home town of Shashone Peak, just north of Rock Springs, Wyoming.

A few months after moving to town, the new parents of a healthy baby boy were both able to secure teaching jobs; Meghan teaching third grade at Westridge Elementary School and Rodger at the high school as a biology teacher and assistant football coach.

Following many years of hard work and tireless commitment, Rodger had become the head football coach and proud leader of the defending two-time state champs.

But right now, none of that mattered. It was just him and the beautiful skyline that he had grown accustomed to. Unfortunately, he had become so lost in his own thoughts, that his phone vibrating in his pocket had gone unnoticed.

Walking to his beloved dark green Dodge Ram pickup, he removed his phone from his jacket pocket, checking the time. He immediately realized his error in judgment when the eight missed calls from his wife flashed on the screen. Before he dialed home, Rodger decided to check his lone voicemail and find out exactly what he might be walking into.

"Why the hell do you have you goddam phone on silent again? How many times do I have to tell you not to do…" Meghan's voice was still ringing in his ear as he set the phone on the passenger seat. The message would continue for another two minutes, concluding with a very

straightforward statement, *"If you are not here in the next ten minutes I will drive down there and drag you home by your ears!"*

Knowing that his wife was not the kind of person to throw out idle threats, Rodger began the long journey home. Taking one last look at the picturesque, peaceful horizon, he prepared himself for what he could only imagine was World War III.

ꋏ

Rodger pulled his truck into the driveway, immediately noticing the gaping hole where the front window once sat. He got out of his truck and walked over to the open hole in the wall. As he picked through the glass shards that remained stuck in the window pane, Rodger could feel his blood begin to boil. "Now what the hell is this?"

Finally beginning to understand the reasoning behind Meghan's meltdown, he brushed the glass off of his hands and charged the front door, prepared to enter the fray.

Having worked up some scenarios in his head prior to entering, Rodger was not ready for what he saw after he stormed through the front door. Sitting calmly next to one another at the dining room table were his daughter Emily and son Sam, both covered in sweat and blood.

Sam was sporting a black eyes and a nasty cut on his left cheek, while Emily seemed mostly unscathed except for a small bandage covering her left nostril that trickled blood.

The expressions on their faces told the story of what had occurred after the obvious fracas. Their heads were slightly bowed and Rodger could see the puffiness around both of their eyes from tears recently shed.

At the head of the table sat his beloved wife Meghan. Her beautiful blonde hair was now a tangled mess encompassing her face like wrinkled drapery.

Her eyes had a ring of fiery red enveloping the stunning blue, and they pulsated with a repressed anger. She was dressed in coveralls and she still clenched the brush she used in her right hand, the paint long since dry.

Without a word, Meghan looked up at Rodger with a piercing glare that caused him to recoil in fear. With her left hand, she motioned for him to sit at the other end, never uttering a word. Rodger sat across from her, and as he opened his mouth to speak, Meghan raised a finger to silence him. Rodger understood the gesture, and quickly retracted.

Meghan sighed deeply, looking first at both her children then back to Rodger.

"Now that we are all here," Meghan began at just above a whisper, "I think it's best if we discuss the events of our day. Rodger, would you like to begin?"

"I think we ne…," were the only words of protest he could muster before Meghan cut him off with one very defiant word.

"NO."

She stared at Rodger, her hand trembling with anger.

Meghan raised her hand to her brow and pushed back her bangs.

"I want to hear about your day honey," she said in a deceptively sweet tone.

Reluctant at first, Rodger quickly realized it was in his best interest to follow his wife's guidance.

"Umm, well we had a fine practice today. The coaches and I think the defense will be stronger in the secondary this season, which as you know had been or weakness the last few seasons. Unfortunately we need to tighten…," as usual Rodger was getting overly excited about the team to understand that he was digging a very deep hole for himself. As he rambled on, the anger growing within Meghan was about to reach its boiling point, but she patiently waited for him to finish his story.

Finally catching on, Rodger cut short his story mid-sentence and cleared his throat. "So, are you going to tell me what happened here?"

"Why, thanks for asking my love. I would just like to say how pleased I am that your day went so well. Mine, on the other hand, was unfortunately not so pleasant." Meghan brushed the hair from her face and adjusted herself in the chair, putting on a fake smile.

"After you left this morning, I treated myself to a wonderful breakfast out by the pond. From there I took a soothing bath and prepared to finish my latest project in peace."

Meghan looked over at her children, a maniacal grin growing across her face. "I was sitting in my studio, painting, relaxing. Then without warning, a deafening crash echoed through the house. Rushing to the living room, I was half expecting to see a car sitting on our couch, for that could be the only thing that could cause that much of a racket."

With her grin quickly turning into a scowl, Meghan pointed an accusatory finger at Sam and Emily. "But to my surprise," she continued with growing aggravation in her tone, "I find your two children strangling each other on my leather couch. Between the blood and the screaming, it took me a second to notice the hole where our window used to be."

Meghan reached up and wiped a tear from her eye. Composing herself, she looked back at Rodger and raised her hands to the sky. "I just don't know what to do anymore. You're gone all day, while and I'm here trying to keep these two from killing each other. I can't take their constant bickering."

Meghan leaned forward in her chair and pleaded with her husband. "So what I need from you is a little help before I lose what's left of my sanity: can you do that for me, please?"

Rodger stared at his wife, speechless.

Sam looked up from the table and began to speak, but was cut off when Rodger pointed his finger at him, "Not a word from you."

He shifted his attention away from Meghan and focused every ounce of his steely gaze onto Sam and Emily with a quiet fury.

"Now listen and listen good. I have no choice but to be at the school every day for practice, and that means you both are under the supervision of your mother. But, by golly, even though I'm not here, that doesn't mean that I'm not *here.* Do you both read me, or do I need to spell it out for you further?"

Sam and Emily quickly glanced at each other, both trying not to laugh at their father's last statement. Even though he was in his early forties, the kids have always been blown away at his corny way of expressing his anger.

Sensing their lack of focus, Rodger smacked the table in an attempt to regain his children's attention and to stress the importance of the conversation. With a growing inferno now smoldering in his glare, he continued. "Now, for the next three weeks it will be both of your responsibilities to not only work off the costs of replacing the couch and window, but to focus on regaining the trust of both me and your mother."

Rodger sat back and grabbed the side of the table, bracing himself from the backlash of his next statement. "This also means that you both are to give up your cell phones and neither of you are to leave the yard for any reason." As expected, this sent Sam and Emily into hysterics.

Sam leapt to his feet and focused a wave of unbridled fury onto his father. "What! I can't believe you," he shouted while wiping the saliva that has begun to fly from his mouth. "How am I gonna explain this to Cindy? Three weeks apart will be the kiss of death for us. Joe Stafford had already tried to hook up with her when we went to Grandma's last month. I might as well break up with her now and save us both the trouble!"

As Sam laid into Rodger, Emily had turned her full attention to Meghan. "Mom, you can't be seriously okay with this. I'll literally die without my phone. This is beyond unfair!"

For the few moments Rodger and Meghan let Sam and Emily vent their frustrations. When he had enough, Rodger stood and gently tapped the glass in front of him with his fork. The sudden noise drew Sam and Emily's attention back towards their father. Understanding the purpose of her father's action, Emily sat back down while pulling Sam back into his chair along the way.

Rodger stared into the eyes of his two children. "Now that I have your attention, let me say one more thing." Towering over Sam and Emily, Rodger lowered his voice to barely a whisper, trying to increase the effect of the next few words. "I am not asking you to do this. You ARE grounded, you WILL give up your phones and you WILL obey every word your mother and I say to you. Is that understood?"

Realizing the futility of voicing any more objections, Sam and Emily sulked down in their seats, both defeated. Sam, teeming with repressed rage, looked over to Rodger. "Can we be excused please?"

"Up to your room for the rest of the night," Rodger demanded. "I will have a list for you in the morning with your first day's chores."

Sam was first to rise, followed by his sister. As they made their way out of the dining room, Sam turned back towards Rodger and Meghan and said the three words that all parents dread hearing, "I hate you."

Chapter
Two

The reality of the situation and the severity of the punishment that Sam and Emily would face throughout the next two weeks had become apparent to the children early into their sentence.

As they were being roused from their peaceful slumber four hours earlier than normal, Sam and Emily received their list of chores.

Today they were to mow the lawn, trim the bushes around the entire yard, clean up the remaining evidence of their battle royal from the previous day, and finally, today and every day was to end with them sitting together for an hour of conversation and play; but there was to be no TV or video games. Their time would be spent communicating directly with one another. This was the final slap in the face from their parents, and an obvious ploy to force them to bond.

Emily was surly as she ate her cereal, but Sam was strangely optimistic during his breakfast. After powering through his meal, he took command of the sheet and delegated out the punishment, taking the majority of the physical labor for himself. Emily was to stay in the house and clean up the mess from their fight, while Sam took it upon himself to tackle the yard work. Emily was curious why such a lazy slob like Sam would burden himself with the majority of the chores, but she didn't argue.

Now, Sam was not stupid or overly charitable. Before giving up his phone, he was able to discuss his situation with his girlfriend Cindy. Together they set up an elaborate "cloak and dagger" like system of communication, all of which depended on Sam being outdoors for the majority of his punishment.

Living in the four bedroom colonial just next door to him, Cindy was planning on sneaking through the adjacent woods during predetermined times each day, giving them a few precious moments alone to console each other through this difficult time.

With his breakfast now over, Sam raced outside and began his work like a man possessed. Emily on the other hand, trudged her way into the living room where a bucket of soapy water was waiting for her. Unfortunately for her, Meghan was going to supervise the repairs to her sitting room, making Emily's task a thousand times more tedious.

As the day progressed, it became apparent that Sam's deceit was working. He had planned each of his movements with surgical precision. Every time he moved closer to the tree line, his mower would mysteriously jam, causing him to stop and tend to the machine.

This was when Cindy would join him from her spot in the shadows. From their vantage point, Sam could see the entire yard leading up to the house. As long as they remained vigilant, their ruse would never be discovered.

Early in the afternoon, the two young lovers were almost discovered making out, but they were able to avoid detection thanks to Cindy's dog acting as their early warning system. He was well trained and knew his obedience would earn him a belly full of treats.

But their bliss was not meant to last. For as the summer sun dropped lower in the sky, Sam knew that it was time to meet up with Emily for the first of many unbearable conversations. Finishing up his half assed job on the rear shrubs, Sam spent two more minutes in the woods with Cindy, and then headed into the house.

Sam took a quick shower to wash away the dirt and grass he had acquired throughout his day, and then tried his best to cover up the shiny new hickey on his neck with some of his mom's concealer.

Following a brief search of the house for Emily, he found her patiently sitting on the front porch, *Monopoly* already spread out on the table. She smiled up at him as he walked through the front doorway.

"What the hell are you grinning at spaz?" Sam questioned with an irritated curiosity.

Emily just innocently shook her head. Looking over to the poor patch job on Sam's neck, Emily giggled, "So, how's Cindy? Didn't know she was into vampirism; it's kind of kinky."

Instinctively slapping his hand over his fresh love bite, he flopped down into the chair across from Emily. "Go to hell Em," Sam responded with a smirk.

Scanning the table, he pointed to the game, "What's this?"

"Well this is a board game," Emily responded sharply, "this is how people used to entertain themselves before the PS3 came into the world."

Rolling his eyes at her tone, Sam just snorted, "Whatever. Let's get this nightmare over with."

The two spent the first half hour playing in an uncomfortable silence, neither wanting the other to think they were actually enjoying themselves. As the game continued, a small conversation soon overtook them.

Watching the two converse like old friends warmed Meghan's heart. She had been watching them from a small window in the foyer for the last ten minutes, ecstatic that her plan had worked.

An hour into their game, the sound of shuffling feet drew the kids' attention to the road. Focusing on the approaching steps, Sam soon realized that they belonged to Jerry Kerr, an old hermit who lived just north of the high school.

The frail man stood maybe five feet tall and was dressed in the same tattered old suit that he had seemed to wear every day. The material might have seen better days, but it still held the sharp creases of a finely tailored suit.

What little of his silver hair that remained was kept hidden under the brown fedora atop his head. Everything about Mr. Kerr screamed ordinary, except for the silver box he held firm in his brittle hands.

"Hey Mr. Kerr," Sam shouted at the tiny figure creeping past. The fragile, older man turned and waved one of his feeble hands back at the kids.

"Good evening Sam," he replied in a barely audible, weak voice. "Good to see the both of you are staying out of trouble."

"It's easy when you're under house arrest," Emily responded, returning the man's wave.

Smiling, Mr. Kerr continued on his path without further comment. Gradually, he disappeared past the next home.

Emily looked over at Sam, "I didn't know you were so tight with Mr. Kerr?"

Turning his attention back to the game, Sam rolled the dice for his next turn. "You know I've done some yard work for him in the past. In fact he wants me to cut down an old oak tree for him before school starts. He said the branches have started growing too close to the house."

Emily whistled, "I still can't believe how far he walks every day. It must be thirty miles."

"Don't be stupid Em. Cindy's mom is a waitress at the café down the road and she said he likes to walk after he eats dinner. I guess he's in almost every night."

"What do you think is in that box he carries," Emily asks Sam after returning to their game.

"Who knows," Sam mumbled. "Maybe that's where he keeps his stash." Sam moved his fingers to his mouth and mimicked the act of taking a hit off of a joint. This caused Emily to erupt into a fit of unbridled laughter.

Once she regained her composure, the kids spent the rest of their night coming up with even more outlandish theories of what the box might contain.

Over the next two days, time would pass without any excitement. Even though the nature of their chores would change from day-to-day, Sam was still able to find something to do outside each day.

Emily had decided that it was in her best interest to help Sam with his deceit, realizing that keeping him happy would make her life in prison much easier.

Each day would also bring new challenges at the game table. Wednesday's heated game of chess would conclude with Emily partaking in a ten minute victory dance, while Thursday ended with Sam embarrassing Emily in *Gin Rummy*.

Mr. Kerr continued his daily walks, greeting the kids with warm smiles and kind words. Every interaction precipitating further speculation over what the box might contain.

Thursday night the kids were treated to some ice cream and a few sitcoms with their folks. As the family sat quietly in the dark with the images of the TV flicking in front of them, the kids turned towards one another and smiled; both realizing that this punishment might not be as bad as first thought. Unfortunately for them, neither could imagine how horribly wrong they both were.

ဟ

In the early hours on Friday, a rumble of thunder shook the peaceful house. As if from a Bible story, the skies had opened up and a deluge of rain battered the area with an unrelenting ferocity.

The monsoon-like rainstorm flooded the high school fields, causing today's football practice to be cancelled. As a result, for the first time since the "incident", the family would find themselves together for the entire day.

Sam and his father had spent the last few days at each other's throats and were now not speaking, both too proud to admit any fault in the week's events. Sensing that the tension between the two was becoming more intense, Meghan decided to give the kids a day off from their punishment and she treated the whole family to lunch and a movie.

Reluctantly, Sam and Rodger agreed to go, leaving Emily and Meghan no choice but to act as buffers.

In an attempt to keep the peace, over lunch Meghan suggested the family go and see the new Tim Thomerson action movie *Trancers 8: The Path of Deth.*

Immediately this decision would spark a hint of excitement and finally some conversation between father and son.

Leaning over to Emily, Meghan whispered, "Nothing brings boys together like blood and boobs." Emily broke up laughing, never receiving even a glance from the two giddy men.

After two and a half brutal hours of testosterone-filled carnage, the family returned home, Rodger and Sam gushing over the glorious depictions of death and destruction the entire ride.

Noticing the time, Emily asked Sam if he was still up for a game. Realizing the sacrifice she had made all day for his benefit, and the help received from her all week regarding his love life, Sam graciously accepted.

Being his turn to choose the game, he would eagerly retrieve *Stratego* from the basement. Emily was not pleased, seeing that this was the only game she had never mastered.

The daily contest of wits would last a couple of hours, with the outcome staying true to form. Sam once again would rise with his hands in the air, triumphant.

"I am Superman," he proudly announced to the world.

Emily just shook her head at his ridiculous proclamation.

"A super douche is more like it."

After a few more minutes of back and forth insults, they began to clean up the remnants of the game. As he folded up the game board, Sam paused, curious to why Emily kept looking up at the street with concern.

"What's wrong with you?"

Emily shook her head, "I'm not sure, but something's just… off."

Looking over to Sam, Emily questioned, "Have you seen Mr. Kerr today? I don't remember him ever walking by."

Sam looked out over the street. The rain had ended three hours prior and the pavement was almost dry.

"No, I didn't. That's kinda weird," he replied. "Maybe he took a day off because of the weather."

Emily turned and looked at the empty road, "Maybe."

Finishing their task, they both went inside, neither of them able to get over the feeling that something was wrong.

5:42am

Torn from his sleep by a dream he could not remember, Sam found himself awake at a time he normally would just be going to bed. Rubbing his eyes, he stumbled down the stairs and into the kitchen.

After brewing a ridiculously strong pot of coffee, he walked out onto the porch in a daze, half expecting Cindy to be lurking in the bushes.

As he stepped through the doorway, Sam slipped on something. Angrily searching for what caused him to spill half of his coffee, he was surprised to find an envelope on the ground.

Scanning for any sign of who may have left this, Sam was discouraged to find the streets absent of life.

Taking a swig of coffee to clear his head, Sam sat on the top step of the porch, set down his still steaming cup and opened the envelope. Inside there was a folded piece of lined notebook paper and a plain metal key.

Placing the envelope and key on the table next to his cup, Sam opened the paper and was surprised to find a lengthy letter addressed to him and Emily. After scanning the paper front to back, he and began to read its contents:

Samuel and Emily

Something unfortunate has occurred and I am forced to take an unexpected trip. My hope is that while I am away, you will both find time to check in on my belongings. I have many old antiques that I cherish very deeply. I only ask this of the two of you because of Sam's familiarity with my home. I do not have many acquaintances that I can trust and I hope you will both do me this favor.

As you may have noticed, I possess a small, silver lockbox. I am unable to bring it with me on my journey and must also place it in your care. This box and its contents are very precious to me, and I hope you will guard this treasure as if it were your own. I apologize for not being able to give you any more information on what secrets lie within the box, but its contents must remain hidden for your own safety.

You will find the box in the second floor washroom of my home; I have placed it just behind the oak tree.

If for any reason you both find yourself in need of help or answers, you will find assistance at this number; 212-555-8421. Just mention the name Simmons to the contact on the other end and they will know what to do. Please, only use this resource as a last resort and for your own safety, this correspondence must remain a secret.

Thank you both for your help.

Sincerely,

Jerry Kerr.

P.S. Under no circumstances are you to open the box. You have to trust me.

Sitting back in his chair, Sam attempted to understand what he had just read. The cryptic nature of Mr. Kerr's request was only overshadowed by the feeling of dread the letter gave him.

'I can't see why me and Emily need any help watching an old man's belongings,' he thought to himself; and the fact that Mr. Kerr mentioned twice that silence was what would keep them safe didn't sit very well with him either.

He read through the letter one more time then picked up the key from the table. Studying the small metal object, he couldn't help wondering what part it played in this little mystery.

Just then Sam heard the unmistakable sound of his father walking down the stairs. The groans of pain from his bad knees coupled with the occasional flatulence were unmistakable.

Quickly gathering up the key and the letter, Sam hid everything under a loose board in the deck that he had discovered during one of the game sessions he had with Emily. Just seconds after he replaced the board, Rodger poked his head around the corner.

"What are you doing up this early?" he asked curiously.

Sam straightened up and grabbed for his coffee mug. "I couldn't sleep," was all his shocked brain could muster as a response. Pointing to the mug, Sam tried to distract his father's attention' "I did brew a pot of jet fuel, it's in the kitchen."

Rodger responded with a twinge of skepticism in his tone, "Is that why you're so damn twitchy?"

After a few tense moments, Rodger smirked and looked at his son's coffee mug, "Hell, it's probably better than that crap your mom forces on me every day."

The words had just left his mouth when they both heard Meghan's booming voice coming from the stairs, "Hey, I heard that mister," she said in protest, "You'll appreciate my "crap coffee" when you're drinking your lunch through a straw!"

With a quick wink and a smile, Rodger disappeared into the house. Sam could hear his parents laughing as a friendly battle ensued.

Letting out a sigh of relief, Sam knew that this was only the first obstacle that lay ahead for him. Walking back into the house, Sam paused and gave the loose floor board one more glance; it was time he woke up his sister.

ς

Emily wiped the remaining sleep from her eyes. She sat up in her bed and looked over to Sam. He was deep in thought as he stared out of her window at the rising sun. It had been two hours since his discovery and he had spent the majority of that time explaining the details of what had happened to his partially comatose sister.

"Alright," Emily grumbled as she checked the time on her alarm clock, "can you run that by me one more time?"

As stoic as a rock, Sam continued to stare out the window, "I think I've told you enough times already," he replied.

"I understand what you're saying; it's the part where you're trying to make me think this is real, that's what's causing me to question your sanity."

Sam turned from the window and walked over to his sister's bedside. Before he flopped down next to her, he snatched her pillow and smacked her upside the head.

Shaking off the attack Emily howled, "What the hell is that for?!"

"Will you keep you damn voice down? If Mom and Dad hear this they'll screw everything up."

"Jackass," Emily murmured as she climbed out of bed.

She let out a sigh as she stretched her hands to the floor. Not wanting to sit next to her brother, she leaned back against her dresser.

"So why do you think Mr. Kerr chose us for this?"

"I already told you what his letter said. He doesn't really know anyone in town that well, and after the work I've done with him, maybe he considers me a friend."

Emily scratched her head and pondered over their current predicament. "Well, what do you think we should do?"

Sam shook his head and looked up at his sister. "I don't know. Part of me wants to go over to his house today and look around."

Emily chuckled with disbelief, "Are you crazy or just stupid? Do you have any idea of what will happen to us if Mom and Dad discover that we skipped out on our punishment?"

"I don't really care about what they might do; I'm going crazy holed up in this prison, and now this gets dropped into our laps. I'm not gonna just sit here and do nothing about it, and you can't tell me that you're not a little curious."

Emily turned and looked at her disheveled reflection in the mirror. Reaching for an elastic band, she pulled the curly mess of her hair into a ponytail. As she continued to work on her appearance, she asked Sam the million dollar question.

"Well Einstein, how are you planning on slipping past both of them? Mom would be hard enough, but Dad is also home all day today. It's like having two pissed off guard dogs instead of just the one; and the second one is bigger and meaner."

Sam looked at Emily with a sly grin, "I might have overheard them discussing a trip to the gym later this morning. That usually ties them up for at least two hours; should be plenty of time for me to ride to Mr. Kerr's house and back."

Finishing her primping, Emily moved to the bed and stood next to her brother. She paused a brief moment to ponder their options and just shook her head.

"It sounds like a bone-headed idea."

Sam got up from the bed and stretched his arms to the ceiling. "I don't remember ever asking for your approval."

Emily looked at her brothers now exposed belly, "I didn't say you needed it. But you are wrong about one thing."

"Oh yeah, what's that?

Emily quickly punched Sam in the stomach, causing him to double over in pain. As she made her way towards the door, she slapped Sam's back as she passed.

"I'm coming with you.

Chapter
Three

That morning at breakfast was especially stressful. Sam and Emily had spent the better part of the morning trying to plan their adventure while the whole time evading detection from their parents.

As the family sat at the table, eating the burnt waffles Rodger had so proudly made, the two kids exchanged nervous glances back and forth. The suspense of what was about to occur was almost too much for them to handle.

Following breakfast, it was time to begin their daily chores. Today Rodger was having Sam clean out the garage and Emily was tasked with organizing the mass of clutter in the attic. Both had taken to their assigned duties with uncharacteristic vigor, causing Rodger to momentarily question if these were, in fact, his children.

As with every Saturday, Meghan and Rodger prepared for their weekly trip to the *Universe Gym* in town. After giving instructions to Emily, Meghan sent her to the attic, but not before returning her cell phone.

"Now I'm giving this to you in case of emergencies," Meghan cautioned her daughter. "I don't trust your brother because he would be sure to call Cindy and talk forever, so I hope you can be responsible with it?"

"Yes mom," Emily said with a roll of her eyes.

Meghan kissed her on the forehead and left Emily to her work.

Running out the front door, Meghan stopped for a second to check on Sam. "We'll be back around one," she yelled to him.

Sam poked his head out of the garage. "K. Hey, can you pick me up some batteries from the store? My TV remote is almost dead."

"Sure honey. What kind?"

"Triple AAA's please; at least four of 'em."

His Mom waved back in acknowledgment as she ran to the idling pick-up truck. Little did Sam know that this would be the last time he would ever see his parents.

ᕤ

Once their Dad's truck was out of sight, Sam raced up to the attic to retrieve his sister. It only took them a couple of minutes to change into regular clothing and collect the tools needed for their adventure.

With their window of opportunity beginning to slowly close, Emily made one final check of their inventory. "We're set," she shouted over to Sam who was retrieving the key and letter from under the loose board on the deck. After stashing the items into his bag, he joined Emily at the bikes.

Sam went over the plan one more time with his sister just to make sure they were both on the same page. Content, they grabbed their packs, climbed on their bikes, and sped down the road in the direction of Mr. Kerr's home.

Mr. Kerr lived at 617 Lincoln Avenue, which was just a few miles to the south of their home. The two-level structure he lived in was very old and over the years had sparked many rumors of ghosts, vampires and all sorts of grisly murders.

Sam and Emily never went along with the stories, but at the moment, that was all Emily could think about.

She couldn't imagine what they would find inside. Shivering with fear, she kept pushing her bike to keep up with Sam's.

Sam was peddling like his life depended on it, and if they didn't make it back before their parents, it just might.

After twenty long minutes, the kids pulled up to the small colonial. Sam looked at the home with disbelief. Last fall he had helped Mr. Kerr clean up the leaves in his yard, and he had not been back since. To his surprise, the once welcoming home looked like hell.

The lawn was unkempt and growing wild; the once manicured shrubbery now attacked the home with a tangled mess of vines.

Throwing his bike to the ground, Sam carefully stepped over what was left of Mr. Kerr's prized garden gnome collection; each had been broken into a million pieces.

As he made his way up the stairs, he was horrified to find the large steel front door was hanging off of its hinges and covered in dents. As Sam inspected the damage to the entranceway, a sense of dread washed over him. Fearing the worst, Sam motioned for Emily to stay where she was while he made his way inside to investigate.

"You don't have to ask me twice," Emily whispered in agreement as she tossed a flashlight to him. "Just watch yourself."

Sam forced a smile as he clicked on the flashlight, trying the whole time to masquerade just how terrified he truly was.

He turned and focused the beam of light into the shadows lurking inside the home. Past the foyer, the main living room was hidden from sight save for the occasional ray of sunlight that attempted to break through the drawn shades.

After carefully entering the home, he shined his light around the expanse; Sam was shocked to see the tattered remains of what was Mr. Kerr's home.

Slowly moving into the living room, he lifted the nearest shade, revealing just how bad the extent of the damage was. Every piece of furniture was broken and shredded. The classic books from Mr. Kerr's collection now lay on the floor; each page torn from their spine.

"Hello?"

Sam paused and waited to hear a response, hoping it would not come from the perpetrators of this carnage, but the house remained silent.

Moving further down the hall, Sam checked the kitchen and found more of the same. The refrigerator was lying on its side, its contents leaking all over the floor. Sam reached down and touched a head of lettuce at his feet; it was still cold. Whoever did this must have been there recently.

Nervous that they might return with his sister just hanging out up front, Sam called for her to join him.

A few moments passed before Emily appeared in the kitchen doorway. She looked as surprised as Sam was, and even more terrified.

"We need to get the hell out of here," she urged as she tugged on Sam's backpack.

Sam turned to face her, "I agree, but first I need to find the lockbox."

Emily shook her head violently. "Are you kidding me? Screw the box; I don't want to end up like that fridge."

Pulling himself away from her grasp, Sam sped past her and quickly made his way to the staircase leading to the second floor. Taking the steps three at a time, he was at the top before Emily could process what had just happened.

Surveying his surroundings, Sam was not surprised to find more devastation waiting for him. Each room was ransacked and left in ruin. As he carefully moved away from the steps, he found what it was he was searching for. On the left side, just two doors down was what remained of the bathroom.

The door had been torn from the wall and water flowed out into the hallway. Sam turned the corner into the room and was immediately sprayed in the face.

The faucet in the shower had been broken off and water was saturating every inch of the room. Sam grabbed the shower curtain and closed it, keeping the majority of the liquid at bay.

Once the makeshift sprinkler had been stymied, Sam turned his attention to the vanity. Giving it a quick once over, his first instinct was to try to lift it from the wall. With a great heave he soon realized that it was securely fastened to the floor.

Scratching his head, Sam bent down and opened the vanity doors. The inside of the cabinet held the normal plumbing hardware you would typically find under a sink, and nothing else. Sam began to tap around the inside of the vanity, listening for any sound which may lead him to a loose board or secret door; he found nothing.

Frustrated, Sam was about to leave when he saw something that seemed out of place to him. Just to the right of the vanity, there was a small oak tree painted on the wall near the floor. It was at this moment that he remembered the note; *'I have placed it behind the oak tree'*.

Lowering himself to eye level with the design, Sam reached out gently and touched the tree. To his surprise, the design wasn't flush with the wall; it was actually indented in the middle. Sam gently rubbed the tree until he noticed a pattern emerging from beneath the paint.

Reaching into his pocket, Sam retrieved the key that was included with Mr. Kerr's letter. Positioning it just above the tree, Sam inserted the key into the depression.

With a slight turn, the vanity shifted and slowly swung free from the wall. Stunned by his discovery, Sam peered into the void. Safely tucked away inside, resting on a lone shelf was Mr. Kerr's lockbox.

After removing the box from the wall, Sam began to inspect his discovery. It was old, very old. The metal had pockets of rust around the hinges and the handle on top had seemed to have broken off. The box seemed pretty normal, except for what was being used to secure it. In place of the original latch, there was a gold plated, modern combination lock.

This mesmerized Sam. He moved the box around in his hands so to look at the lock from every angle. It was like nothing he had ever seen. The golden lock had seven dials, each covered in strange markings, and the ten symbols on each dial were all different.

Sam was fascinated by the strange symbols; so much so that he almost didn't hear the sound of the approaching footsteps.

Snapping out of his trance, he peered around the corner for the source of the noise, and was surprised to find Emily sprinting up the stairs.

Scrambling to where he was, she stopped just outside of the bathroom. Visibly flustered, she began to shake as she tried to catch her breath.

"Whoa, calm down spaz," Sam said as he put his hand on her shoulder, "What's going on?"

Choking on her words, Emily struggled to reply, "A…A car just pulled up out front."

"Is it Mr. Kerr?"

Emily just shook her head, "I don't think so."

The way in which she punctuated her statement sent a cold shiver down Sam's spine. If it wasn't Mr. Kerr, then who was it?

Following their abrupt exit from the gym, Rodger and Meghan had begun a heated discussion on the drive home. The topic of this argument was about the importance of Rodger not looking at other women while they exercise.

Meghan sat in the passenger seat of the truck fuming while Rodger tried his best to ensure her that he was innocent. "I'm telling you honey, I was only looking at the TV. It was just a coincidence that a girl was on the treadmill just below it."

Meghan remained focused on the road ahead. Every word spoken by Rodger just seemed to bounce off of her icy exterior. Growing increasingly frustrated by the direction of the conversation, Rodger inadvertently put the final nail into his coffin.

"I can't believe you actually think I would look at another woman while you're there!"

The words had just left his lips when Rodger realized what he had said. In a very methodical motion, Meghan turned to face Rodger. Her face was a dark shade of red, and if you looked just right, you may have seen smoke emanating from her ears.

"Get me home," was the only phrase she could muster; but it was enough to make Rodger shudder in fear.

His big mouth once again cursed him to a fate he didn't want to imagine.

Turning onto their street, Rodger noticed something odd. From a distance, he saw two large, black SUVs parked in their driveway. Slowing up a bit, Rodger nudged Meghan.

Infuriated by his touch, Meghan snapped, "I don't want to talk about it anymore!"

Unfazed by her response, Rodger continued to survey their home as they approached. "It's not that," he said, "There seems to be a party at our house."

Turning her focus to the house, Meghan could now see what had sparked Rodger's curiosity. After scanning the house, she had noticed a couple of men dressed all in black lurking around their yard.

"Who the hell are those men looking in our windows," she questioned.

Rodger just shrugged.

"Rodger," Meghan asked as a wave of panic washed over her, "what about the kids?"

Fearing the worst, Rodger stepped on the gas, sped past the blocked driveway and barreled into the front yard, just missing the large oak that stood adjacent to their driveway.

The sudden commotion drew the attention of the two men and they drew their assault rifles, sights set on the large truck.

Shocked by the sudden display of firepower, Rodger put the truck in park and dragged Meghan under the dashboard.

"Lower your weapons," a voice shouted from across the yard.

From their position under the dash, Rodger sneaked a peek at what was happening.

In the distance, the rear driver's side window on the lead SUV was going up. The door suddenly opened and a man exited the vehicle. He raised his hands in a symbol of surrender and slowly approached the truck.

Rodger never took his eyes off of the intruder. The man was of medium height and build, but he carried himself with unquestionable confidence. Like his men, he wore a black suit and black sunglasses; the only distinguishable trait being the blue pocket square sticking out of his jacket pocket.

He was Caucasian, but his skin was a deep, dark bronze; definitely not a spray tan. His hair, which was pulled back into a well groomed pony tail, was dark amber with a hint of grey.

The man continued to approach, stopping three feet from the truck. Lowering his hands, the stranger removed his sunglasses and placed them in his jacket pocket. He then slowly opened his jacket to reveal a badge of some kind. Rodger did his best to read what was etched in the metal, but the windows were beginning to fog from their nervous breathing.

"Mr. and Mrs. Lana," the stranger shouted in a slight French accent, "I am with the FBI. Can you please step out of the vehicle; it is very important that I speak with you."

This statement added to the tension in the vehicle. Meghan grabbed Rodgers arm and squeezed with all her strength. "What is he talking about Rodger?"

Rodger just shook his head, never taking his eyes off of the dark presence standing in his yard.

"Well," Meghan questioned, "What are we going to do?"

He took a deep breath as he pried his wife's hand from his arm.

"Stay here."

Rodger opened the door to the truck under light protest from Meghan. Peering around the yard, he was anxious to see that there were now two groups of men standing on opposite sides of the house; all weapons pointed at the pick-up truck.

Recoiling back behind the door, Rodger pointed to the two new men he saw and yelled a command towards the mysterious leader. "I don't know who the hell you are, but if you want to talk they need to lower their weapons."

The agent looked around at the rest of his team. With a sudden, stern arm motion, the men all lowered their weapons and walked towards the two SUVs.

Looking back at Rodger, the leader once again opened his jacket, revealing his badge.

"Mr. Lana, I am Agent Johnson of the FBI and this is an emergency. May I please approach the vehicle and show you my credentials?"

Feeling more confident now that the weapons were no longer pointing at him, Rodger stood up straight and moved out from behind the door. "Yes, but you better do it slowly."

As Agent Johnson approached the truck, Meghan reached out and squeezed Rodgers right hand. He looked back at Meghan and just winked. She always loved his confidence, but now she was uneasy about the situation and resented the gesture.

Agent Johnson walked up to the door and removed his credentials for Rodger to review. Extending his arm, Rodger accepted the ID and looked over it silently.

He studied the man's paperwork before passing the ID to Meghan who also gave it a once over. After she was convinced that Agent Johnson was legit, she sat up, shimmied out of the door and joined the two men. Handing Agent Johnson his ID back, Meghan began the interrogation.

"Where are my children?"

Agent Johnson shrugged at the question as he returned his ID's to his jacket pocket, "I was hoping you could tell me Mrs. Lana. We arrived ten minutes ago and there was no answer at the door. That's why we began circling the yard; my men were looking for any movement inside. It appears no one's home."

Concerned about the whereabouts of the kids, Meghan abruptly left the conversation and walked towards the house, leaving Rodger with the agent.

Agent Johnson watched every step Meghan took towards the house; tracking her movements like a hunter after his prey. Noticing this aggressive gesture, Rodger tried to divert the focus back on him.

"Now can you please tell me what the hell you're doing here and what you want with Sam and Emily?"

Agent Johnson looked back towards Rodger with a compassionate glare, trying his best to gain his trust.

"I am here to ask your children a few questions about one of your towns residents; an older gentleman that goes by the name Kerr. We have reason to believe they might be in contact with him."

Rodger gave a curious look, due to the accusation and because of the look of disdain that Agent Johnson had when mentioning Mr. Kerr's name.

"Mr. Kerr? What do you want with that crazy old man and why do you think our kids have anything to do with him?"

"We don't know yet, but there are some who live in this town that believe your children may know him better than you think. Some of you neighbors have heard them talking to Mr. Kerr just this week. Now I wouldn't call that a coincidence."

Rodger was able to muster a nervous laugh, "My wife told me she heard them shout out a greeting as he walked past, but I don't think that makes them best friends."

Agent Johnson looked into his eyes, the glare causing Rodger to cringe.

"Now you wouldn't lie to me Mr. Lana, would you?"

Rodger fought through his fears and became enraged at the insinuation. Standing to his full height, Rodger jammed his finger into Agent Johnson's chest.

"How dare you come to our home; scare us half to death with your goons; make wild accusations about our children, and then question our honesty. I'm sorry but I'm going to have to ask you to leave, now!"

The insult was not lost on Agent Johnson. He just smiled and shook his head.

"I was hoping that you would just have cooperated with me, but now I guess we are going to need to have a more "structured" discussion."

Agent Johnson looked over at one of his men and gave a nod. The man walked into the house and shut the door. From outside you could just make out the muffled yelp of someone being restrained, and then all went silent.

Panicked, Rodger pushed past Agent Johnson and began to move towards the front door, desperate to protect his wife from the trap they had walked into. As he moved closer to the house, Rodger lost all focus as he shouted his wife's name.

"Megh…," was all he could get shout before five hundred thousand volts of electricity stopped him dead in his tracks. Rodger crumpled to the ground, his body violently shook for a moment then it became still.

Agent Johnson looked around the scene as he placed the Taser back into his pocket. The street was still, not a soul in sight. He was glad they had stopped at the neighbors' homes already and silenced any potential witnesses.

Fixing his tie, he motioned for the three remaining men to join him. When they converged on his location, he gave very strict orders.

"I want you to take Mr. Lana inside and make sure he is put with his wife. It's time we find out exactly what they know."

The men nodded in acknowledgment as they performed their task; dragging Rodger's unconscious body into the house.

Now alone, Agent Johnson took one final look around the quiet neighborhood; slicking back some loose strands of hair, he let out a deep sigh.

There was a time in his life that he would have enjoyed a town like this; quiet, picturesque, a living, breathing Norman Rockwell painting. Unfortunately for the people of Shoshone Peak, now he would just have to take pleasure in watching it burn.

He turned from his spot and began the slow walk into the house, the shadow of death following him inside.

Chapter

Four

An ominous, black Buick LaCrosse sat motionless in the drive-way. Its engine continued to idle; the passengers remaining hidden behind the heavily tinted glass.

Sam and Emily remained glued to the upstairs hall window, occasionally peering over the sill just enough for them to see, but not be seen.

It had been ten minutes since the car had pulled up to the house, but to Sam it had felt like an eternity. After Emily had informed him of their company, Sam had placed the lockbox in his backpack before he had taken up his current position next to his sister. It was their intention to wait out the visitors, and maybe keep their presence a secret.

That's when it hit him; the bikes were right in front of the house! Now terrified and trying furiously to think of a solution, Sam's mind was racing with multiple scenarios. He just prayed that the car was full of Jehovah's Witnesses and that they would leave a pamphlet at the door before driving away. He would have no such luck.

As the powerful engine shut down, the doors on the luxury car swung open. Two men of equal size and weight stepped out, both were giants. The driver and his passenger wore dark suits and black sunglasses.

The driver had long blonde hair which hung loose over his shoulders, and his flawless skin was as pale as a ghost.

The equally intimidating passenger was completely bald with a large tattooed skull adorning the back of his head.

Even though both men had to exceed six feet in height, the driver had an authority and grace that was lost on the hulking passenger. The blonde man was clearly in charge; this was obvious.

After a brief inaudible exchange, the blonde man pointed at the bikes in the lawn. The two men looked around, both leaving a hand resting on something hidden within their jackets.

On chance, the passenger happened to look up at the kid's window just as Emily stretched too high for a peek; they were spotted.

The tattooed man shouted to his blonde partner, who also looked at the direction of the children, smiling as he drew his weapon.

"Damn," was all Sam could muster as he grabbed Emily and dragged her into the far bedroom at the end of the hall.

Now sobbing uncontrollably, Emily looked to her big brother for answers.

"Wh..what are we gonna do? They'll kill us Sam. They'll kill us!"

Covering her mouth, Sam pulled Emily to the floor as he locked the door.

"Quiet. They don't know what room we're in and it could buy us some time."

Sam was trying his best to remain calm, but he had also started to shake as the tense situation became overwhelming.

Looking around the room for answers, the sound of footsteps began to echo from downstairs. The men were in the house and it was only a matter of time until they found where the kids were hiding.

As the unmistakable sound of guns being cocked rang throughout the house, a booming voice called up from the first floor, "Hello mystery guests."

A few minutes passed without a response, causing the man to become agitated. "Now that isn't polite. I'm just looking to talk to you. I promise that we won't hurt you…much."

The footsteps grew louder as the two men ascended to the top of the stairs; it would only be a matter of minutes before they were at the door to the bedroom.

Frantically looking around, Sam spotted the window adjacent to the large desk in the corner of the room. Just outside of the glass was a large oak tree, and the wheels began to turn wildly in Sam's head.

Leaping to his feet, Sam grabbed Emily and dragged her to the window. Opening it, he was disappointed to see that the distance to the nearest branch was too great. Looking down at his sister, Sam decided that there wasn't another option, it was this or nothing.

"Here's what we need to do; I'm going to throw you out the window and you're going to try to catch that branch there." Sam pointed to a large branch about ten feet off of the ground, and ten feet from the window.

Emily looked up him in disbelief, "Are you insane? I can't catch that."

Sam had already begun lifting her against her protests.

"We don't have an option here Em. It has to be this."

"Well what about you," she grunted as her body was being forced out of the second story window, "You can't make that jump."

"Sure I can. I'm Superman, remember?"

Emily looked into the face of her brother and knew this wasn't going to end well for either of them, but she trusted him with her life.

Sitting on the ledge, Emily's feet dangled freely over the long drop. Sam whispered in her ear, "It's going to be okay. I'm going to push on three; I want you to shove off of the ledge with all your strength. Okay?"

Emily nervously shook her head in acknowledgement.

"One…two…three!"

On three Sam shoved Emily with all his might. She was able to get a solid push off with her legs, and it propelled her towards her target.

The branch almost snapped under the weight of Emily crashing into it, but it held and so did she. Her arms were cut up and bruised, but she had made it. From her branch, Emily safely dropped the final ten feet to the ground.

Amazed at her journey, Emily looked back up to the window; searching for her brother. Sam was nowhere to be seen.

Not thinking about the importance of remaining silent, Emily shouted, "Sam! SAM!"

Just then their two backpacks flew out of the window, followed by her brother. He was fully extended as he fought against gravity; but even with all of his effort, he would come up just a few inches short of the branch.

Flailing wildly, Sam crashed down to earth with a dull thud. Emily looked on in horror as he lay motionless. She raced to his side just as the blonde man's face appeared at the window.

"Why hello there little birds," the blonde man shouted from his perch. "Now I need you both to stay put until my friend gets there. He will be more than happy to make sure you're okay."

Emily looked down at Sam's lifeless body, hoping for some sign he was all right; that's when she saw his eyes. he was blinking ever so subtly; just enough for her to notice.

"Make for the woods on my signal," he whispered through clenched teeth.

Too afraid to argue or question him, Emily just squeezed his hand in acknowledgement.

With the approaching footsteps of the tattooed stranger growing louder, Sam bolted to his feet. Catching the blonde man by surprise, Sam was able to grab the two bags and Emily before the gunshots began sounding from behind.

The tattooed man had appeared from around the corner of the house as the bullets began to fly. Charging after the kids, his Luger roared to life as he focused his fire towards the fleeing children.

The kids zigzagged the entire way towards the dense tree line just behind the house, narrowly escaping the rounds that whizzed by their heads. Breaking through the first row of low hanging branches, the kids could hear the anger laced profanity coming from the blonde assailant and his partner.

Praying that the larger men were as slow as they looked, the kids ran as fast and as far as their legs would take them, traveling deeper and deeper into the dark labyrinth that was Hamilton Forest.

5

Groggy from the shock of the Taser and what had come after, Rodger tried his best to shake off the cobwebs. Following the initial attack, Agent Johnson's men had taken turns beating him. They never asked him any questions, it seemed like this was done out of pure enjoyment.

Trying his best to survey the area through his swollen eyes, it didn't take him long to realize that he was in the laundry room of his basement. Unfortunately he was not alone; tied up next to him was his beautiful wife Meghan. She sat motionless, her golden locks now stained red with blood.

Rodger attempted to stand, only to come to the realization that he also was strapped to a chair. He strained against his bonds with as much force as his weakened state could muster, but to no avail.

"Meghan," he cried out in anguish.

She remained still.

"Meghan!"

There was a twitch from her head followed by a weak grunt, then nothing.

Rodger rested back into his seat; a small sense of relief washed over him knowing that she was alive.

Behind him, the door to the room opened. Rodger fought against his restraints as three sets of footsteps approached.

"Who the hell is back there? What do you want from us?!"

A large hand hit Rodger across the mouth, knocking out two of his remaining teeth.

Adrenaline now pumping through his body, Rodger was quickly able to recover from the attack and focus his attention on the blurry form standing in front of him.

A familiar voice now echoed through the tiny room, "There is no need for that kind of language Mr. Lana."

With just that short exchange, the memory of the man who now spoke came rushing back to Rodger; and so did the bitter grip of gut wrenching terror.

Agent Johnson sat down in a chair facing the two captives. He contorted his neck from side to side until a loud crack interrupted the silence; followed by a pleasurable sigh.

Looking back over at Meghan, Agent Johnson signaled to one of the two guards who had followed him into the room.

"Anton, will you please wake up Mrs. Lana?"

The large Russian shook his head, *"Da, ser."* Ignoring Rodgers protests, he walked over to Meghan and shook her violently.

"Keep your filthy hands off of her yo…," was all Rodger could get out before another large hand crushed his jaw. His head lagged to his chest as this last attack stunned him to the point of unconsciousness.

"We need him conscious you idiot," Agent Johnson shouted in a scolding tone.

"Sorry sir," the henchman whimpered in a broken German accent.

"Now wake him up; and this time you better watch that temper of yours. This is a conversation that we will not have again."

Agent Johnson wiped a splash of blood from his mirror black Oxfords with disgust. Johnson, being a well-kept gentleman, hated this barbaric part of the job. He would much rather watch the carnage from afar while sipping on one of his favorite Bordeaux, maybe the '82 Lafleur.

"I think it would be wise to gag them for now, just until we have their undivided attention."

"Yes sir," Holger shouted as he motioned to his counterpart. The men ripped some strips of cloth from shirts hanging on the wash line and tied them around the mouths of Meghan and Rodger.

"Now let's try this again, shall we?"

Agent Johnson looks over to the sink adjacent to the washing machine.

"Maybe try some water instead of causing them any more head trauma. I have learned that getting information from a turnip can be very difficult."

Holger and Anton retrieved two wash tubs that were left under the drop sink. Filling both with ice cold water, the two men approached their prisoners and proceeded to douse the two with the liquid.

Meghan was the first to jump with shock, as if she had awoke from a bad dream. She looked around frantically as she fought against her restraints.

Seconds later, Rodger snapped back to life, spitting the water from his mouth and choking on both the gag and his own blood.

Agent Johnson cleared his throat, "Now I do not have the desire to hurt you any more than I already have, so can we please dispense with the heroics?"

Meghan and Rodger looked up at Agent Jonson and then to each other. Meghan had tears of both terror and fear running down her face; Rodger's initial anxiety had since been replaced with a seething rage over the abuse his wife had taken at the hands of their captors. Both of her eyes were swollen and bruised; her nose was obviously broken, and it continued to bleed profusely.

"It's good to see that you are both finally realizing the severity of the situation you are in. Damaging you like this was not my intention, but after your rude welcome, it was necessary."

Rodger looked back at Agent Jonson and began to shout muffled obscenities. Holger raised his fist once again to strike Rodger, but Agent Johnson stayed his hand.

"STOP," he shouted as he pulled his sidearm. "I warned you once already; the next move you make towards this man will be your last."

Holger recoiled in fear, nodding his acknowledgement.

Agent Johnson returned his weapon to its holster and resituated himself across from the bound couple.

"Now Mr. and Mrs. Lana, I will allow my friends to remove your gags, but only if you both remain calm. This situation does not need to escalate any more than it has; and let me remind you that your children's lives are at stake. Their fate is now in your hands."

Rodger and Meghan both shook their heads in acceptance.

Agent Johnson motioned to Holger and Anton. The two men removed the gags from the prisoners. Content with this small luxury, both captives stretch their jaws and let out a small groan of relief.

Rodger looked over at Meghan, "Are you okay?"

She took a large breath, "Yes, I'm okay. I love you so much."

"I love you too baby. We'll be all right."

"Touching," Agent Johnson replied sarcastically.

Rodger looked back at him and calmly began the next round of dialogue.

"Who the hell are you and what do you want with our kids? I doubt you're FBI."

Agent Johnson smiled at the insinuation, "Yes, I believe we can dispense with the illusion. We are not with your government. Who we are is unimportant; what we want is the only thing you need worry about."

Agent Johnson leaned forward in his chair, stopping just a few inches from Rodgers face.

"It has come to our attention that your children may be in possession of something that my employer desperately wishes to obtain. More specifically, a map that will lead us to something bigger than anything you could possibly imagine."

"What are you talking about? Why do you think my kids have anything to do with your map? I'm telling you, you're wrong."

Agent Johnson leaned back in his chair, "Now do not be so hasty Mr. Lana. We are not working off of a hunch. It took us a great deal of time and cost quite a few of your neighbor's their lives to come by this information."

Rodger and Meghan both recoiled in shock and disbelief, "What are you saying?" Meghan questioned, her voice now trembling.

"Well, we knew the general location of our item, but not exactly where to find it. After spending some personal time with some of your fellow citizens, we came across your son's little lady fair. Alas poor Cindy didn't hold up too well under Holger's interrogation techniques. Your son's name was the last thing she said before…, well I don't think we need to get into the messy details."

"No!" Meghan screamed in agony before Anton silenced her with a firm slap across her face.

Rodger began to strain against his bonds when Holger slammed him back down into his chair.

"Now let's not get out of hand again," Agent Johnson scolded, "You don't want young Cindy's sacrifice to have been in vain."

Seething with anger, Rodger relaxed his shoulders; never taking his eyes off of his wife. Her head lulled side to side in a haze of consciousness.

"What do you want us to do? We don't know where the kids are," Rodger hissed through his broken jaw.

Perking up with excitement, Agent Johnson smiled at the couple.

"Lucky for you, I do! When you were unconscious, I received word that your children were seen fleeing the home of the very man you claim meant nothing to them. Two of my men were at the location, when they were surprised by your dear children.

Unfortunately, the two youngsters were able to escape into the woods just adjacent to the property. It is believed that they removed the item I seek from the home, and I would very much like to retrieve it as soon as possible."

"It can't be true," Meghan mumbled as she fought against her restraints, "Sam and Emily had no reason go to there and take anything."

"Well, I will have to disagree with your assessment Mrs. Lana. It seems that Sam has had interactions with my Mr. Kerr in the past, and that he recently came into the position of correspondence from him."

"Who is this man?" Rodger demanded.

"He is someone who I would very much like to meet, but that is not why I need to find your children. What's important right now is that I retrieve the item they stole before my men find them. You see, they don't possess the same level of restraint that I do."

This statement terrified Rodger and Meghan. It became clear that the situation was not going to have a happy ending.

Crestfallen by this realization, Rodger reluctantly agreed. "What do you want us to do?"

Rising from his chair, Agent Johnson once again retrieved the 9mm Berretta from under his jacket. He folded his hands in front of his belt, making sure the couple had a good view of the weapon.

"I actually don't need anything from you Mr. Lana; it's Meghan who will be of assistance. I assume your children own cell phones."

Shocked by the appearance of the gun, Meghan nervously nodded her head, "Emily does."

"Good. Now I need you to call her and say exactly what I tell you."

Raising his weapon, Agent Johnson placed the barrel against Rodger's forehead.

"Or I'm afraid poor Rodger may lose his head."

After running through the forest for what seemed like an eternity, Sam and Emily collapsed to the ground exhausted. Emily looked behind them for any sign of their pursuers, but they appeared to be alone. Relieved, she slumped down onto a fallen tree and began to break down.

"Hey, you need to be quiet," Sam whispered.

"What…*sob*…is going on? Who are those men and why were they shooting at us?"

Sam leaned up against a large oak tree, favoring his left shoulder.

"I don't know. It seems like they were looking for something."

Sam glanced over at his backpack; curious about what lay inside.

"Can you bring me my bag?"

Wiping away her tears, Emily grabbed his bag and brought it to him, the whole time staring at his arm with concern.

"Here," Emily said as she handed him the pack, "Are you...*sniff*... okay?"

Sam accepted the bag with his right arm, wincing with pain as he moved.

"I think I might have dislocated my shoulder in the fall, but I'm not sure."

"Can you move it?"

"Not really, but it'll have to wait until we can figure out what's going on."

Emily stood over her brother as he lifted the lockbox from his bag. Moving it around in his hands, Sam was discouraged by the complicated combination lock sealing the container.

"Damn."

"What is it," Emily questioned.

"There's some kind of lock on this thing, I don't remember ever seeing a combination anywhere in the house or in Mr. Kerr's letter to us."

Slamming the box back into the bag, Sam let out a grunt of agony as he attempted to stand.

"This is starting to piss me off. How could Mr. Kerr get us involved in this crap?"

"Maybe he didn't know this would happen."

Looking at his sister in disbelief, Sam just laughed.

"Oh, so you think we just happened to stumble on a couple of thugs in nice suits robbing an old man's house? Grow up Em; this is bigger than a simple robbery."

"Don't talk to me like that, I'm not stupid," Emily shouted, "I'm just trying to think of reasons why we're all of a sudden running for our lives."

"Alright! Just keep it down."

Sam looked around the dark, damp woods in which they were finding sanctuary.

"We don't know where those pricks are and I think it would be better not to be here if they catch up."

"Okay," Emily reluctantly agreed, "What now?"

"We need to find help." Sam pointed west of their position, "I'm guessing we're close to the sheriff's office. If I'm right it should just be a mile or two in that direction."

Sam looked around before resting his glance on Emily's bag.

"Did you bring your phone?"

"Yes, but I don't have a signal here. We need to get out of the woods."

"Okay, but we need to keep hidden. I don't want those assholes finding us."

Sam collected his bag and slung it over his good shoulder. He walked over to Emily and placed his hand on her shoulder as she collected her belongings.

"I know this sucks, but we'll be alright. We just need to get ahold of mom and dad. They'll know what to do."

Wiping back her tears, Emily looked into her big brother's eyes, "Mom will kick their ass for what they're doing to us."

They both let out a soft chuckle over her statement. A temporary reprieve from the fear of their situation; and something they both needed.

Chapter

Five

"**What's** the problem?" Agent Johnson remained steadfast, his gun barrel pressed against Rodgers brow. Holger looked at the cell phone he was holding with a confused expression.

"I not getting signal sir. The lady in phone saying other phone not in service."

"Give me that," Agent Johnson demanded.

Holger handed his boss the phone. Agent Johnson fumbled with the touch screen, never taking his gun hand away from Rodger's head.

"Their phone must not be in range."

Agent Johnson handed the phone back to Holger, "Keep trying; and you really need to work on your English. You sound like a buffoon."

"Yes sir," Holger said as he took back the phone; within him burning a repressed hatred for his employer and his snide remarks. Holger's intellect surpassed that of Agent Johnson's, but that was a debate he would never win.

Just as Holger began to redial Emily's number, the phone suddenly began to ring. Emily's name and picture appearing on the caller ID.

Agent Johnson looked at Meghan, "Our luck has changed. Remember what I said," he threatened as he pulled back the hammer on his gun.

Meghan shook her head vigorously.

Holger placed the phone on speaker just as it connected.

The temporary moment of silence was interrupted by a shaky voice on the other line, "*Mom?*"

"I'm here baby," Meghan said, trying to remain calm.

"*Mom, something terrible is happening. Sam and I need help! There are strange men shooting at us and Sam is hurt, and we don't know what to do!*"

Meghan looked over at Agent Johnson as she spoke in a calm, robotic tone, "Calm down honey, tell me what's happened."

There was a muffled sound on the other end, and then Emily's voice was replaced by Sam's.

"Mom, are you and dad alright?"

"We're fine Sam; we're just worried sick about you two."

"Why do you sound so funny? Where's dad?"

Agent Johnson pressed the barrel firmer into Rodger's forehead, "Speak," he said in a soft, but commanding tone.

"I'm here Sam. Everything's okay."

The other line remained silent. Worried about blowing this opportunity, Agent Johnson kicked Meghan's chair and motioned for her to continue.

"Are you still there honey," Meghan questioned.

"Yeah, were here." This was followed by a short silence and then Sam asked a question that gave everyone in the room pause, *"What should we do?"*

Realizing Sam understood what was happening, Meghan looked over to Rodger. She stared longingly into his eyes. The many years of love they had shared was about to come to an end in this world; hopefully it would be carried on into the next.

They held each other's glance for only a moment, but the silent message of love that was exchanged could have filled a thousand lifetimes.

Meghan looked up at Agent Johnson's confused expression and just smiled defiantly.

"Run baby! Run and never st…," was all she could get out before an ear piercing crack interrupted her thought.

The call had ended.

Meghan sat in shock as the smoke still rose from the fresh wound that sat between Rodger's icy blue eyes. Her soul mate was gone. The life together that she had cherished so much was over.

Meghan let out an anguished, blood curdling howl. Her pain was unbearable; it was as if her heart had been ripped from her chest and thrown into the fire.

Agent Johnson looked on with sick satisfaction. The pain Meghan was feeling seemed to fill him with unbridled joy. Holger and Anton looked away as they knew what was to happen next. The two soldiers couldn't help but shed a tear at the sorrow felt by this petite warrior.

Agent Johnson wouldn't need any further help from Meghan and Rodger to find the children; the GPS signal from Emily's cell phone was enough to track them down. Now he was just satisfying his salacious appetite for pain and suffering. It was all a game to him, and now it was time to make the final move.

Without even speaking a word, Agent Johnson turned the gun on Meghan ending her torment with one quick flex of his finger.

$$\mathcal{S}$$

Sam and Emily sat behind a large blue trailer home just off of West Ave. They had left Hamilton Forest only moments ago, emerging south of a large trailer park.

As they exited the tree line, Emily's phone began to vibrate; there were two missed calls from their mother. Excited about the possibility that their parents were going to save them from this nightmare, the kids feverishly dialed Meghan's cell phone; unaware of the danger they were putting themselves in.

The conversation would only last a few seconds, but the effect of the call would change their lives forever.

Sam sat motionless; the cell phone still resting in the palm of his trembling hand.

Emily began to shake Sam violently. Terror over what she just heard now washing over her in a wave of emotion. "What was that!? Sam," she shouted in agony, "What just happened!?"

He remained silent. A lone tear trickled from his eye. The shock of what occurred was fully understood by this stoic, heartbroken child.

"Sam! Look at me!"

Sam looked up at his sister's face, knowing that she was all he had left in the world. Swiftly moving from his seat, Sam embraced Emily with all the strength he could muster from his one good arm. Holding her close, he began to weep.

Barely able to speak, he was able to manage a few simple words, "They're gone Em."

With the truth of his words sinking into her heart, Emily let out an ear shattering scream. She buried her head into Sam's chest and released all of her anger and sorrow into him. Her small frame shook uncontrollably with grief.

The two held each other tight, sharing in the moment of monumental lose; the rest of the world disappearing around them.

Seconds later, the sound of tires screeching around the corner broke Sam from his trance. He quickly jumped to his feet, wiping the tears from his eyes. Looking around the corner of the trailer, Sam could see a black luxury sedan pulling up to the home. It was a Buick LaCrosse.

Sam ran back to his sister, who still remained balled up on the ground sobbing. Falling to his knees next to her, Sam began to shake her with his right arm, his left still hanging limp at his side.

"Emily! Emily! They're here. We need to go, NOW!"

Emily's limp form stirred, but remained dormant. "I...I don't want to run anymore."

Sam grabbed her face and looked into her red, swollen eyes. "We don't have a choice, we need to run! I will not let you get hurt."

"But Mom and Dad are dead!"

"We don't know that for sure," he lied. "But if they are dead, they died to protect us. Mom and Dad gave us a chance to survive, and I will not let anything happen to you. We need to keep fighting; for them."

Injected with a sense of purpose, Emily arose from her shell and wiped the tears from her eyes. "Where are we going to go?"

Sam slung his bag over his shoulder and grabbed Emily's hand.

"I don't know, but we won't give up without a fight."

Chapter

Six

It was another glorious summer day in Shoshone Peak. Sheriff Ethan Cole was heading into the office a little later than usual.

Normally a punctual man, the Sheriff was still a little hung over after the wild bachelor party he attended the previous night for Deputy Bob.

His 1996 Eddie Bauer Edition Ford Bronco slowly puttered down Main Street. This truck was his baby. It was jet black and in mint condition, with the exception of the small dent left in the driver side door by his ex-wife. The woman couldn't cook to save her life, but she sure could swing a baseball bat at a moving car with deadly precision.

Shoshone Peak had been his home for the last fifteen years, and at forty-six he had no plans of ever leaving. The first decade of his law enforcement career had taken place on violent streets of Oakland, California. Following that hell, this peaceful setting suited him just fine.

The morning commute was as nice as any he could remember. The friendly people of the community traveled from shop to shop, smiling and waving to each other.

The local PTA had set up a bake sale in the church parking lot, hoping to raise enough funds to send the senior class to Washington, D.C. next year. Yes sir, life was good.

Breaking the peaceful silence, his radio that hung from the dashboard suddenly crackled to life, *"Sheriff Cole? Come in Sheriff."*

Reaching for the receiver, the Sheriff sighed as he took one last pause to look at the beautiful skyline. "This is Sheriff Cole. What's going on Reggie?"

"Trying to shake off the Jack Daniels you were feeding me last night sir. My head feels like hell right now."

"I know what ya mean," he said as he adjusted his sunglasses. "I'm getting too old for that kind of party."

"You could have fooled us Sheriff. We didn't know you could pole dance."

Shaking his head, Sheriff Cole just laughed. "If anyone finds out about that I'll lock up the lot of ya and deputize those dancers."

There was some laughter from the other end followed by the sound of a pill bottle being shaken.

"So what's with the call Reg; we could have reminisced when I got to the station."

"*There was a call just now from Mr. Burdick over on West. He said there were a couple of terrorists firing cannons in his back yard.*"

"And you believed that old nutter?"

"*Not really, except that we received a few other calls about someone firing off fireworks near there. It might just be a coincidence, but it all sounds kind of fishy to me. Thought you might want to stop over on your way and check it out.*"

Sheriff Cole checked his watch.

"It's just past noon. Have any of the others checked in yet?"

"*Just Bob so far sir. I sent him out to a call on Liberty Drive. Jay Connolly was passing through the neighborhood when he saw two men fighting in Rodger Lana's front yard. It sounds like some sort of domestic disturbance had broken out.*"

"Keep me informed on that situation, I'll try to check in as soon as I figure out what's spooking Mr. Burdick."

"Roger that Sheriff."

The line went dead. Now alone once again with his thoughts, Sheriff Cole turned down East Elm St. and into the fray.

Deputy Bob Galindo inched down Liberty Drive, his head throbbing with a dull ache brought on from dancing and multiple liters of cheap bourbon. Last night the boys threw him one hell of a bachelor party, and he still felt a little drunk. Lucky for him, Sheriff Cole should be a lot worse off after his little pole dance with the girls, and probably wouldn't notice.

Scanning the block as he crept closer to his destination, Bob searched for any sign of a problem. But the street seemed eerily deserted. It was a beautiful eighty degree day and there wasn't a cloud in the sky, but not a single child was playing; nobody was out in the sun washing their cars, it looked like one of the episodes of the *Twilight Zone*. Something was wrong, but what?

As Bob approached Coach Lana's house, he began to get concerned. Rodger had been a close friend for the last five years. After he had coached Bob his senior year at Jefferson, he had helped Bob get into college and eventually pulled some strings to get him his job with the Sheriff's department. Hell, he even introduced Bob to his fiancé Jen. This man and his family were good people, and Bob would do anything for them.

As he pulled up to their home, Bob became suspicious when he saw the two large SUVs parked out front. He also noticed Rodger's truck now sitting in the lawn, the driver's side door wide open. Puzzled by this, Bob pulled behind the trucks and fired up his sirens.

To his dismay, three large armed men exited the home followed by a well-dressed, tanned gentleman. The smaller figure walked slowly over to the vehicle with his arms up, hoping not to spook the young officer.

Bob opened his door and drew his weapon as he exited the vehicle.

"Now that's close enough mister. Who are you and where are the Lana's?"

The stranger stopped a few feet from the deputy, "I am truly sorry for this confusion officer; I am Special Agent Johnson of the Federal Bureau of Investigations. I have come here in search of a very dangerous fugitive. The Lana's were assisting me and my colleagues in capturing this fiend."

"Let me see some identification."

Agent Johnson reached into his coat pocket.

"Hey," Deputy Bob shouted with concern, "Not so damn fast. Take your hand out of your jacket slowly."

Agent Johnson obliged, removing his hand from his jacket in a very gentle motion.

He opened his badge, passing the ID to the deputy. Bob quickly reviewed the document, his weapon remaining aimed at Agent Johnson's chest.

"You see officer, we're the good guys."

The deputy closed the badge and lowered his side arm as he passed it back to Agent Johnson. As he accepted the ID into his right hand, Agent Johnson swiftly removed his own weapon with his left and placed a round squarely between Deputy Bob's eyes; dropping him where he stood.

"That was too easy."

Agent Johnson holstered his sidearm as he approached the car. Admiring his handiwork, he gave Bob's corpse a little kick.

"I could have probably tricked this hayseed with a plastic star and some crayons. God I love Americans."

Spitting on the deputy's face, Agent Johnson turned to his men.

"Gentlemen, can you please escort the deputy's body inside with the others? It is time to leave."

Agent Johnson focused his attention back to where Holger was fidgeting with a detonator, "Are all of the preparations for our departure set?"

"Yes sir," Holger grunted, "I make sure myself."

"Excellent. Well, let the party begin."

Agent Johnson walked back to his SUV and waited for Holger to open his door; begrudgingly the large German handed his boss the detonator and opened his door for him. After shutting the door to the vehicle, Holger turned towards the house and whistled to his fellow agents.

The men exited the house and they all loaded into the two trucks. As they sped away from the house, Holger could hear Agent Johnson counting from the rear. "Three... Two... One... boom."

Just as he finished his count, there was a deafening explosion and the Lana home was engulfed in a ball of flame. Like dominos, the neighboring homes also disintegrated into a wall of fire and debris.

The quiet neighborhood was no more. What remained was a fiery hell of which nothing and no one could have survived.

ᔕ

Sheriff Cole was just a few blocks from the origin of the disturbance call when his truck began to shake violently. Checking his rear view mirror, he was shocked and terrified to see what grew off in the distance. A massive cloud of glowing smoke and fire climbed into the midday sky, enveloping the sun in a choke hold of darkness.

Caught in a sudden rush of horror and total disbelief over what he was witnessing, the sheriff forced himself to turn his attention back to the road. As he refocused on his driving, a blur caught his eye just in time to slam on his brakes. The mighty Bronco skidded to a halt, only inches from the two individuals who had just stumbled into the road. Before he could get out of the truck and find out what the hell was going on, his passenger door flew open and the two figures jumped inside.

Caught off guard by the sudden move, Sheriff Cole reached for his gun. As he was about to draw, he recognized Samuel Lana and his sister Emily; they were trembling uncontrollably as they cowered on the passenger seat of his truck.

"Samuel Lana! What in the hell do you two think you're playing at."

Sam looked at the sheriff, a fresh coating of blood across his cheek. "Drive! Now, they're right behind us!"

"Now just wait one damn minute. Who's right behind you and what in the hell happened to you?" Before Sam could respond, a flurry of bullets riddled the idling Bronco.

"Jesus H. Christ almighty! Hold on you two!"

Sheriff Cole popped his truck into gear and hammered down on the gas pedal with all of his might. The large vehicle lurched forward and quickly gained momentum. As they fled from the attackers, more rounds punctured the rear of the vehicle, breaking out windows and shredding the rear seat.

Sheriff Cole crossed over to the next block and turned north, back into town. When he was sure they had lost the gunmen, the sheriff grabbed the radio and immediately screamed into the mouthpiece.

"Reggie!"

The line remained silent.

"For Christ sake Reggie, pick up the friggin radio!"

As if on cue the radio sparked to life, *"Sheriff Cole... I repeat, come in Sheriff Cole. This is an emergency."*

"You're goddamn right it is! I have just been fired upon by unknown assailants. I don't know who the heck they are but they were gunning for the Lana kids. I have them right here with me and it looks like they've been through a war; over."

"Sir, there has been a massive explosion over on Liberty. It looks like the whole street has been destroyed."

"Destroyed? How the hell did this happen?"

"I'm not sure; it's still hard to comprehend."

"Is there anyone you can get out there to see what's going on? Wait, isn't that where you sent Bob off to?"

"Yes sir, but I haven't been able to reach him since the explosion. Jen's here scared to death and I don't know what to tell her. As far as the rest of the deputies, I haven't been able to get ahold of them either. Something big is going on sheriff and I'm scared shitless."

"Now just calm down Reggie, I need you to relax and do your damn job. Start by finding the others and then try to figure out what the hell happened on Liberty. We'll be there soon"

"Sorry sheriff, I'll keep it together. Wait...I think someone just pulled up, I'll get back to ya."

Emily realized what she just heard and turned to her brother terrified, "Liberty, Sam that's our street!"

Sheriff Cole looked over to his two passengers, "Will one of you tell me what the hell is going on?" Having finally scanned the terrified children, Sheriff Cole was surprised to see the extent of their injuries. Sam favored his left shoulder; a piece of his right ear was missing, causing the large amount of blood now covering his face.

Emily was just covered in blood and dirt, but it didn't seem like the blood was from her wounds; it was probably just rubbed off from her brother.

Sam looked down at his grieving sister, "We don't know sheriff. Everything just began to melt down around us. I...I think those men killed our parents." Just saying the words caused him to choke up; he hadn't yet had time to accept what took place.

"Well we need to get to the bottom of this." Sheriff Cole keyed up his radio once again, "Reggie, you still there?"

The other line was silent. Frustrated by the lack of a response, Sheriff Cole began to shout into the mouthpiece but was cut off.

"I'm here Ethan. What's your location?"

Sheriff Cole paused when he heard the greeting; Reggie never called him Ethan over the radio, he was always respectful of the badge. Something wasn't right.

"I'm heading to the station now, have you been able to reach Deputy Galindo yet."

"No sir, he still hasn't checked in yet. I had my girlfriend Jen put a call out to his wife, but Barb hasn't seen him either. What's your ETA?"

Just as the Sheriff feared, it seems that Reggie and perhaps the whole station had been compromised. The kid wasn't the sharpest tack in the box, but he certainly knew how to communicate under pressure after watching all of those blasted *Law and Order* shows.

"Sit tight Reg. I'll be there in a minute; I just have to make a stop first."

"Good luck boss," was the last thing Reggie said before the line went dead.

Sheriff Cole immediately turned west and stepped on the gas; distancing them from the town.

Sam looked up at the Sheriff; he was confused with their change of direction.

"Where are we going sheriff?"

Sheriff Cole just looked straight ahead. His face was now a mix of sadness and rage; a stream of tears rolled down his cheeks.

Growing irate from the lack of a response, Sam raised his voice, "Why aren't we heading back to the station?! I don't get it."

Somber, the sheriff just kept looking forward, "There isn't a station to go back too. Whoever is causing all of this mess has taken control."

Sam sat back in stunned silence. He now understood the impact of the conversation between the sheriff and his deputy.

"I'm so sorry sheriff."

The truck motored on down the road until it reached the highway and from there they turned south onto Route 191.

Sheriff Cole wiped his eyes from under his sun glasses, "We need to get you to a hospital. I have a doctor friend in Rock Springs who can help patch ya up. Just stay down and keep still till we get there."

The Bronco picked up speed as they roared down the highway, the rest of the ride remained silent, save for the sobs of grief over the memory of those lost to the day's senseless destruction.

Reggie's corpse was thrown on top of the pile now building in the department's lone holding cell. Agent Johnson had his men stack the remains of what little resistance they had faced, including Jen, the young twenty year old bride-to-be. The remaining police force of Shoshone Peak put up little resistance, and they all met with the same terrible fate.

Pacing back and forth in front of his fully assembled six man team, Agent Johnson reviewed his options.

"I believe our simple friend over there was able to warn the sheriff to stay away from this building, and I think it has worked. Now is the time that we need to put our best foot forward and discover the destination of the sheriff and our map."

He continued to pace in silence for a few minutes before coming to a stop in front of the agents who pursued Sam and Emily. Folding his arms, he glared at the two men who now hung their heads in shame.

"But before we go on, I need to decide what to do with the two of you."

In an act of sheer cowardice, the tattooed man fell to his knees and pleaded for mercy from Agent Johnson.

"Please sir, we tried our best. Franc and I chased those little bastards all over the town. We had them until the police pulled up. I swear that next time they will not get away."

Agent Johnson leaned in and placed his arms around the large man's head, pulling him into his chest. "I completely understand Karl. It was a fluke event that could have happened to anyone, even me." As he consoled him, Agent Johnson removed a small knife from under his shirt sleeve and with a quick strike, plunged it into Karl's cerebellum. Karl's body spasmed for a brief moment before going limp, the life draining out of him through the new hole at the base of his skull.

Agent Johnson held onto Karl long enough to feel the last twitch of life leave him, and then he pushed the man's lifeless body to the tile floor.

Turning to address Franc, he wiped his knife off on a Wyoming state flag hanging from a nearby wall.

After he slid the knife back into the sheath he had strapped to his hip, he rested his hand on Franc's shoulder, "Now, are you as much of a coward as poor Karl, or are you willing to accept the blame for this abysmal display of incompetence?"

Franc remained still, his expression stoic even though he now began to tremble with fear. " I… There is no excuse for our actions. I take full responsibility for the mission's failure."

Agent Johnson methodically addressed the large man standing before him; a sadistic smile growing across his face.

"Franc, you are an idiot," he said as he playfully slapped the man's face, "but I applaud your humility."

As Franc relaxed his body, Agent Johnson leaned in so that only Franc heard his next few words. "But if you ever disappoint me again, I will not be as charitable."

He released Franc and addressed the rest of his men, "Now, before the young deputy over there passed on, he mentioned that the sheriff's truck was not loaded with a GPS transmitter, so tracking him will have to be done the old fashioned way."

Looking around the station, his eyes rested on the sheriff's office.

"Holger; I need you to search the sheriff's office for any sign of where they may be heading, and who the sheriff trusts. Names, addresses, anything we can use."

Holger snapped to attention, "Yes sir," he then turned and headed for the sheriff's office.

Agent Johnson approached Franc, who was still shaking from his slim escape from death's clutches. Grabbing Franc by the chin, he pulled him within an inch of his face. "Are you ready to redeem yourself young man?"

"Ye…s sir," Franc replied, his voice shaking with fear.

He released Franc and motioned for Anton to join them.

"I have chosen to believe poor Karl's assessment of the children's physical state; meaning that they will most certainly be seeking medical attention for the boy. I am sure that the sheriff is not careless enough to risk admitting them to the local hospital, but nonetheless, I want you both to stake out the town's hospital and search for any sign that they may have been or are still there. Understood?"

"We will not fail you sir," Franc shouted with a renewed vigor.

"I'm sure you won't," Agent Johnson sneered, "But stay extra sharp. Our fireworks display earlier has probably left the locals with a slew of wounded. The hospital might be full."

Without another word, Anton and Franc both exited the station as fast as their feet could carry them, both now fearful of what the penalty would be if they failed.

The two remaining men had remained stuck at attention, petrified by fear. The taller of the two was easily six foot seven and his skin was almost as black as the suit that draped over his lanky frame. What little hair that remained on his head was shaved into a tight fade, small traces of white peppered throughout.

The second man stood no more than five and a half feet, but his immense muscularity could be detected through his suit. He appeared to be Middle Eastern in descent, but there was a hint of African ancestry in his features.

Agent Johnson approached the taller man, "Tau, I need you and Amun to break into every hospital database within two hundred miles of this location and I need it done yesterday. Now can you both handle this task, or do I need to motivate you as well?"

Tau stood up straight, his head barely missing the low hanging ceiling fan above him, "It will be a piece of cake sir."

The men stared at each other for a brief moment before Agent Johnson broke the uncomfortable silence.

"What, do you need an invitation? GO!"

"YES SIR," the two men shouted before scurrying away like scared mice.

Agent Johnson collapsed into the desk chair just behind him, "Why am I surrounded by such unnerving incompetence?"

He playfully spun the chair a few times, stopping face-to-face with a picture of Sheriff Cole dressed like Elvis from the previous year's Halloween party. "What do we have here?"

Studying the photo, he began to laugh. "The king is dead." In a sudden motion, he punched his fist through the frame, shattering it into thousand pieces. Reenergized by the thought of finishing this assignment and once again reaffirming his dominance over any who cross him, he stood and straightened his jacket. "Long live the king baby."

Chapter

Seven

Twenty minutes had passed since Sheriff Cole's Bronco pulled up to the hospital in Rock Springs. Upon entering, he was able to admit Sam under a false name; he still didn't know who he could trust at this point.

Sam and Emily had been sequestered in a private office near the back of the emergency room, where Doctor Jesse Shultz was now busy wrapping Sam's arm up in a sling. The sheriff had left them in Jesse's hands while he tried to gather any information he could about what had happened in the town just an hour ago. Curiously, the rest of the world seemed ignorant of the events that had taken place. Crestfallen over his lack of answers, Sheriff Cole rejoined the group. "So how are the patients, doc?"

Doctor Schultz looked up from his work, "The young lady has some minor cuts and bruises. Sam here has had a more productive day. He has a micro fracture in his left clavicle and he's missing a piece of the right pinna."

"Pinna?"

"That's what we like to call the top of the ear, Ethan," Jesse responded sarcastically.

Sheriff Cole just rolled his eyes. He had grown up with Jesse back in Pahrump, Nevada; a small town just west of Las Vegas. Even though their dreams of dealing cards at Caesars Palace would never come true, the two would remain close friends after high school. It was through a personal connection that Jesse had with Sheriff Cole's predecessor in Shashone Peak that would eventually bring Ethan to Wyoming.

"Funny Jess, real damn funny. Sorry, I never had a taste for *Grey's Anatomy*."

Sheriff Cole walked over to Emily, who was sat next to Sam's bed. She was motionless; her expressionless gaze focused on the multicolored tile floor.

Sheriff Cole brushed back some loose, bloodstained strands of her hair, "You alright sweetheart?"

Emily sniffled, but remained still.

Sheriff Cole just shook his head. He couldn't imagine what the children had gone through. Overcome by the emotions stemming from his own loss today, he didn't know how to express his feelings of immense sorrow and sympathy for the children's plight. Turning towards Sam, he playfully swatted at his sneaker, "How you holding up Sam?"

"I don't know sir," Sam answered, "I just can't believe what's happening. Do you know anything about who did this?"

The sheriff sat at the foot of Sam's bed, "I couldn't find anything on the news or the internet about what happened. It's very strange. Usually a town doesn't get attacked like this without someone noticing; and please Sam, call me Ethan."

Looking over to Jesse, the sheriff motioned towards the door, "Can ya give us a couple minutes Jess?"

"Sure Ethan. I'll be right outside if you need me."

As Jesse walked towards the door, Sheriff Cole called out to him, "And remember Jess, we're not here."

Jesse winked back to Ethan, put his left index finger to his lips and walked out of the room.

After Jesse left the room, Ethan turned back towards the kids. "Now I need you both to tell me once again exactly what happened today. Don't leave out any detail; every piece of this puzzle is important."

Sam shifted in his bed and began to tell the story from the beginning. After he had finished, there was a small whimper from Emily. Turning to her, Sam noticed a small tear running down her cheek. As he reached over to touch her she pulled away in disgust.

"Don't you touch me," she snapped and turned away from Sam. "This is your fault! I hate you."

Sam slowly pulled back his hand; the guilt he felt was clear.

"Now stop that," Ethan shouted to Emily, "This was not Sam's doing. The bad guys are out there, not in here."

Emily kept her back to the men, her sobs muffled by her sleeve.

After removing his hat and rubbing his head, Ethan turned back towards Sam. "I can't figure out why these men are after you, but it must have to do with what you've got in your bag. Can I see it please?"

Sam reached over to his bag and removed both the box and letter. He handed them cautiously over to Ethan.

After spending some time looking over the box, Ethan placed it on the bed and focused on the letter. He read through it a couple of times and put it down on top of the box.

Sam looked on with curious excitement, "Well? What do you think?"

"I haven't the foggiest. Maybe if we could get into this box we could figure something out."

Sam sat up a little straighter in his bed, "Should we call someone?

"Who do you think we should call?"

"I don't know, maybe the State Police or FBI."

"I think it would be best that we don't broadcast our whereabouts. At least not until we figure out who is looking to hurt the both of ya. These men just mowed through my entire police force with ease. Only well trained folk could have done this, and men like that usually are connected through the nose."

Reaching down and picking up the letter, Ethan studied the number written near the bottom, "Have either of you kids tried calling this number?"

"No," Sam replied, "We didn't have a chance since all of this started."

Rubbing his chin, Ethan recognized something about the number, "I'm no expert, but this looks like a New York City area code."

"Should we call it sheriff?"

"Well, I don't think we have many options left, do you?

ʕ

Outside Grand Central Station
New York City
1:10pm

Joe Pagano sat next to the newspaper stand he had called home for the last twenty years. He had never been too crazy about this town or the trash he tried to sell to every commuter racing past him, but the *Enquirer* did help to pay the bills. At 57, he was too old to leave New York; especially when his beloved Yankees looked like they might actually put a decent pitching staff on the field this year.

Joe had come to New York in the nineties, hoping to start a new life for himself. After chasing bad guys across the globe since he was a teenager, Joe felt that New York was the best place to disappear.

He had spent the remaining few dollars he had left from his days with the CIA to buy this stand; and it had been his home ever since. It wasn't a bad life. Sure the pay sucked, but he was able to flirt like a sailor with every attractive woman that walked by; and other than his tattered Yankee's cap, Joe was still a looker. He stood just a hair over six-foot and he kept up his physique by lifting weights at the local rec center. He may have been on the downward slope to sixty, but he didn't look a day over 35.

Today had started like all the others. Joe had met the morning commuters with a smile and kind wave, receiving mostly scowls in return.

Jason Schwartz was his best customer, and he had stopped at the same time he always did to buy his morning copy of *The Daily News*. He was a good kid; he worked at some big shot lawyer firm near Wall Street. Too bad he was a Mets fan; Joe always held that against him.

After the morning crew had disappeared in a rush, Joe was left with nothing but his thoughts and a couple of stragglers. Fortunately, the silence wouldn't last long; once the clock struck noon the streets filled again, this time with hungry people looking for the best street vendors in the city.

Joe was lucky enough to have *Derek's Taco Heaven* parked next to him every afternoon. *Derek's* was always a big draw, and having that much foot traffic helped Joe sell some papers.

After the lunch crowd scurried back to their buildings, Joe took up his spot next to the stand. He loved to feel the sun beat down on his face; it reminded him of his time in Baghdad.

As the afternoon sun started to sink in the sky, Joe began the daily checklist that he followed before closing for the day. That's when he was interrupted by a sound that made his heart stop. A cell phone he had stashed in his bag began to ring. Now this was no ordinary phone; this phone never rang before, and there was only one person in the world who knew the number.

Jumping to his feet, Joe ran inside and lowered the wooden screen he used to secure the stand when he closed up shop. Now isolated from the world, Joe removed the phone and stared at the call ID. Confused over the number on his screen, Joe answered the line, "Hello?"

The other line was silent, but Joe could hear the soft breath from whoever had reached out to him.

"Who may I ask is calling and how did you get this number?"

"*I'd rather not say who I am, but I can tell you this number came from Simmons,*" a masculine voice uttered from the other side of the call.

Upon hearing this, Joe froze in disbelief. This was a call he had hoped would never come. "Are we speaking on a secured line?"

"*Not really. I'm calling from a hospital phone; I would assume it's not encrypted.*"

"Is the package secured?"

There was nothing but silence on the other end.

"I repeat; is the package secured?"

"*We have the box.*"

Taking a deep breath, Joe felt a momentary sense of relief. Reaching over to his bag, he removed a laptop and fired it up. After entering in a dozen security codes, Joe began furiously typing. "Now listen carefully, have you been contacted by anyone pertaining to the package?"

"*I would say that. There were about a half dozen men that stormed though my town and left it in ruin.*"

"Can you describe them?"

"*They looked like feds, but I seriously doubt they were. I'm also not alone. There are two kids with me who were caught up in this mess as well.*"

"What kids? Never mind, we need to get you three out of Wyoming."

"How in the hell do y…"

"Don't worry about how I know this; you need to leave, now! These men are not to be trusted or underestimated. I would bet anything that they know where you are and they will find you."

"What should I do?"

Joe looked at his watch, "You need to get out of there and find shelter until I can come and get you."

"Why should I trust you? You could be one of them."

"Trust me, if I wanted to harm you, I could have destroyed the hospital you're in with a push of a button."

"Jesus."

"Now I need you to listen carefully." Joe brought up Wyoming's map on his laptop and reviewed the landscape. "You need to find a way out of there. I want you to find a phone somewhere, preferably a secured landline, and call me back for more instructions. I will expect your call within the hour; and remember, do not trust anyone."

Joe slapped his phone shut. Jamming the laptop and whatever money he had from the days sales into his bag,

Joe looked around the small newspaper stand with a bit of sadness; he knew this was the last he would ever see of it.

♋

Ethan rehashed the entire conversation to Sam and Emily. Following a brief deliberation the three decided to act on Joe's warning. Emily was the first to speak up with an idea for their escape. She thought they should devise their plan based off of a book she had read since she was little.

She loved spy novels and remembered her hero Janice Lancer from the *Dark Sunrise* series being stuck in a similar situation. Janice was on assignment in Egypt when she found herself pinned down by Iranian terrorists.

After some quick thinking, she used misdirection to open an avenue of escape. Using her satellite phone Janice called in a bogus SOS to her agency, knowing her pursuers were monitoring her communication. When they followed her ghost north towards Cairo, Janice slipped onto a train heading west.

Since neither Sam nor Ethan had thought of a better option, the three used Emily's idea as a blueprint in concocting their own escape plan.

Just after arriving at the hospital, Ethan had spent a few minutes searching for escape routes, just in case they needed to make a quick exit. It was during this walk that he found the main dispatch area for the hospital's Mercy Flight helicopter. The station was unmanned at the time, and he took it upon himself to "borrow" the keys for the chopper. He had taken a few lessons back in'07 and it seemed like a good idea to have multiple options available.

Their plan was to have Jesse leave the hospital in Ethan's truck as the group escaped in the chopper. Jesse knew this could end in not only his arrest and subsequent termination, but potentially his death as well; but he would do anything for the man he referred to as his brother.

As Ethan poked his head out of the room to call for Jesse, he noticed a very tan, slender man in a black suit flirting with the lovely young woman behind the reception desk. The man had long salt and pepper hair pulled back into a ponytail, and he was flashing a fake smile along with an even faker FBI badge.

Skeptical, Ethan paused at the door. To his terror, the man held up a picture of Ethan posing with Jesse and the ten point buck they had taken down just last year. Ethan knew exactly where that photo was in his office and the people who were the last to have access to it.

Quickly, he turned to the kids, "Plans have changed. Go, now," he whispered as he pointed to the rear door connecting their room to the next ward.

Without hesitation, Sam grabbed his bag, jammed the box and letter back in and made for the door, followed closely by Emily and Ethan. Slamming through the doors, they ran as fast as they could down the hall. Passing a side door out to the parking lot, Ethan motioned for them to stop and peered out the tiny window. Parked just past the handicapped access ramp was a large, black SUV. The window was down and a large, pale man with a long blonde ponytail sat patiently. His eyes scanned the parking lot; a cigarette smoldered in his large hand.

Ethan quickly pulled his head back and looked farther down the hall. About fifty feet from their spot was a service door with a sign over it that read "ROOF ACCESS".

"There, go," Ethan prodded the group in a hushed tone.

Following his direction they made their way through the door, and quickly ascended the stairs. When they reached the top, Ethan once again halted their movement and peered through tiny window in the door.

The roof seemed barren except for the hospital's Medevac helicopter resting in the center.

From behind, they heard shouting and the rattle of machine gun fire; it seemed the agents were done with asking questions and had moved onto aggressive interrogations.

Ethan looked down at the terrified kids, "Alright you two. When I open the door I want the both of you to make for the chopper and buckle yourselves in."

Sam looked at Ethan in disbelief, "Do you know how to fly one of those things."

"I used to. We'll just have to see how much I remember."

Emily nervously grabbed onto Sam's right arm; squeezing tight.

"NOW," Ethan shouted.

Sam and Emily kicked open the door and ran full sprint towards the helicopter. To their relief, they made it without being shot at and they dutifully went about securing themselves in. Ethan was not far behind; he had hung back long enough to jam a fire axe he had found into the door lock.

Jumping behind the pilot stick, Ethan fired up the helicopter and strapped himself in. After checking on the kids, he began to lift off. Just as the landing skids had cleared the pad, a loud crack echoed over the rooftop.

In a cloud of black smoke, the door to the roof exploded open and three men came rushing out. The first man through the door was the slender stranger Ethan had seen flirting at the receptionist desk; the next man was another agent in a black suit, this one had a blonde crew cut and a pretty nasty scar across his face. The blonde man was dragging someone behind him, and it was the sight of this person that caused Ethan to recoil in shock.

Jesse was forced to his knees in front of his heavily armed captures. The momentum of his forward motion caused him to collapse into a crumpled mound. His coat was tattered and bloodstained; both of his eyes now swollen shut. Shaking off the fall, Jesse looked up at Ethan and just smiled.

"Go already," he yelled in one last defiant move.

As the final syllable left Jesse's lips, gunfire from the blonde man's machine gun ripped through his chest.

"No!" Ethan painfully howled.

Franc looked up from his fresh kill to the helicopter hovering above, smiled and raised the weapon. There was a deafening rattle as the rifle roared to life.

Ethan yanked back on the stick and gave all his effort to clear the roof. The large machine grunted against the sudden ascent, gun fire peppering the windshield and frame. Sam and Emily ducked down as best they could, as glass and metal exploded all around them.

With a desperate jab, Ethan was able to gain enough altitude to turn the old bird away from their attackers. As the chopper continued to climb, Ethan could not shake the image of his oldest and dearest friend being torn down.

The eyes of Jesse's attacker kept flashing through his mind. These men were sadistic on a level he had never seen; it was as if they were amused by the execution. This realization caused Ethan to feel something that he hadn't in a very long time, fear.

Chapter

Eight

After a short flight, Ethan set the massive helicopter down; it had been forty-five minutes since their escape from the hospital. They had traveled northeast then circled back west, landing in the middle of a desolate canyon in the Seedskadee National Wildlife Refuge. This wasn't the most ideal of landing zones, but the chopper had taken damage during the attack and Ethan had no choice.

Still in shock over the loss of his friend, Ethan was silent as he helped Sam out of the back. Emily had already stepped out and vomited profusely. Once they were able to compose themselves, the group spent the next few minutes camouflaging the helicopter the best they could with branches and leaves from around the area.

After completing their improvised helicopter disappearing act, the trio looked around at the empty vista. Scanning for any sign of life, they set out in search of help. The hour was getting late and they had a phone call to make.

In the brutal mid-day sun, the twenty-five minute walk seemed like an eternity. Eventually the battle scarred and road weary travelers stumbled upon an empty ranger station. After checking to see if the coast was clear, Ethan posted Sam and Emily around the perimeter as lookouts. Using some skills he picked up in his youth, he easily picked the lock and entered the station.

To his delight, there was not only a phone but also keys to the four-wheeler parked on the side of the small building. After a brief call to Joe, Ethan grabbed the keys and tried to cover his tracks the best he could; they didn't need any more pursuers.

Collecting Sam and Emily from their posts, Ethan fired up the all-terrain vehicle and drove off as fast as he could with the two passengers hanging on.

Ethan drove south, traveling far enough to feel safe from being discovered if the ranger returned and noticed the missing vehicle. After hiding the ATV, Sam rushed everyone into a cave he found while surveying their temporary safe haven.

Emily collapsed onto a soft patch of moss that covered a large area of the dark cavern floor; she was asleep almost immediately. Ethan and Sam both sat against the cool cave walls, each sighing with relief after escaping the oppressive heat.

Following a period of welcomed silence, Sam tossed a rock at Ethan's foot, surprising the dozing sheriff. "So, what's the plan?"

Ethan wiped the sleep from his eyes, still slightly hung over from the previous night's party, "I was able to speak with our new friend, and he's on his way to meet us."

"Where at?"

"He said to be at the Greater Green River Intergalactic Spaceport by ten tonight."

"Why the hell are we meeting there?"

"He said it's the most desolate place near us that he can land."

"What is he picking us up in, the Millennium Falcon?"

"How the hell am I supposed to know Sam? Maybe he is."

Sam rested his head back against the wall as he ponders this new development. "Do you trust him sheriff?"

"I don't think we have a choice. I mean it seems we've lost every friend we have to these assholes." Resting his head against the wall, Ethan's eyes fluttered shut. "And I told you already, call me Ethan," he said to Sam, "I'm not the sheriff anymore; not since they destroyed our town."

With that final statement, the cave fell silent. Sam was the only one who remained awake. He fidgeted with his sling as the pain has gotten worse after their most recent escape; he wished they had borrowed some more of that morphine he was given at the hospital. Left alone with his thoughts, Sam finally let the true scope of the day's events sink in; the silence temporarily broken by the gentle whimper of his sobs. Today Sam became the man of the family, and he was living an adventure right out of a spy novel; but right now he would trade it all for the comfort of one of his mom's hugs.

ᔕ

Greater Green River Intergalactic Spaceport
10:12pm

Since arriving at the desolate airfield, Joe had spent his time pacing impatiently. His small Cessna Citation Mustang remained fired up and ready to go at a moment's notice. He had landed eighteen minutes prior, and to his dismay, the sheriff and his companions were nowhere to be seen.

The abandoned runway was eerily quiet in the darkness, save for the hum of the Cessna's engine. Joe had his night vision binoculars and he nervously scanned the horizon for any sign of his passengers.

He was about to give up hope when a small vehicle appeared in the distance. It looked like an ATV, but from this distance it was too hard to tell. The one thing Joe became certain of almost immediately was that it whatever it may have been was indeed speeding his way.

As the vehicle sped closer, Joe was able to make out two passengers hanging onto the driver for dear life. Peering behind the ATV, the reason for their high rate of speed came into view. About a mile back from the small vehicle, there were three large SUVs hot in pursuit.

"Gotta go," Joe said as he ran towards the small jet's open hatch. Settling in behind the wheel, Joe brought the plane around and started taxiing towards the oncoming vehicles. As he approached the ATV, Joe slowed to a crawl and flashed his lights.

The small vehicle skidded to a stop and the three occupants leapt from the ATV and ran for the open hatch. The SUVs were now less than five hundred feet from them, and closing fast.

Looking back at his new cargo, Joe shouted out orders, "Shut that damn hatch and buckle up!"

Not waiting for affirmation, Joe steered away from the oncoming trucks and fired up the twin jet engines. As the small plane began to pick up speed, the sound of gunfire rattled off of the rear of the Cessna. Not wanting to test the durability of his new "borrowed" toy against the effect of bullets, Joe punched it and the jet roared down the runway, lifting off into the air.

As the plane disappeared into the night sky, Joe let out a deep sigh of relief. It has been far too long since he had seen this caliber of excitement, and he didn't miss the stress. Setting the autopilot, he stretched his arms and rose from his seat. He had guests to welcome and a lot of questions that needed answering.

As he made his way back to the small cabin, Joe was shocked to find the barrel of a gun pointed at his forehead. Ethan had been waiting for him with his own set of questions, "Who the hell are you?"

Joe was shocked by this new development, but not surprised. "My name is Joe, and I can assure that I am not your enemy. And unless you can fly a plane, I would suggest you put the gun down."

Ethan pulled the hammer back on the pistol, "I'll be the judge of who or what is our enemy, now start talking."

Joe had begun to raise his hands when he relieved the sheriff of his weapon in one blinding motion. Turning the weapon back on the surprised man, Joe held Ethan's gaze. "I'm here to help, and we don't have a lot of time to screw around with this pissing contest." Joe popped out the magazine and expelled the round from the gun's chamber. After disarming the weapon, he handed it back to Ethan. "Now can we please have a seat and talk about the situation. There is much to discuss before we reach our destination."

Ethan accepted the weapon and sat down in the nearest seat, still in awe over what just happened.

As Joe sat down across from them, he scanned the refugees. All three were covered head to toe in dust and mud. The young girl had multiple scrapes over her head and neck which oozed a small stream of blood. Sheriff Cole looked to be in good health, just exhausted. The younger of the two men was in the worst shape. His left arm was hastily tucked into a sling, while his right ear was missing a good chunk; blood seeped through the bandage that was barely hanging onto the ear.

As Joe approached, Sam sat up in alarm. "Easy young fella," Joe said as he motioned for him to remain seated, "My name's Joe. May I ask who you and this young lady are?"

Sam shifted in his seat to a more defensive position, "I'm Sam Lana and that's my sister Emily." Emily looked up and waved in acknowledgement.

"Well it's nice to meet you Sam, Emily." Joe reached for Sam's ear, causing him to recoil. "Sam, I really should have a look at your ear, it looks like it may be infected."

Sam reluctantly accepted. Joe peeled back the bandage, causing Sam to wince in pain.

"Hmm, just as I thought, it's pretty bad. Now stay still and don't touch your ear." Joe moved to the rear of the plane and retrieved a small medical kit. As he sat back down next to Sam, Joe opened the box and removed some bandages and a small vial of liquid. "I need to clean this wound and give you a shot of antibiotics. Now I also have a small dose of morphine, which I could give you if you wanted."

Sam perked up at the news, "I'd most definitely be okay with that."

Joe looked over to Ethan for permission, and Ethan just nodded his approval. Retrieving the small syringe from his kit, Joe jabbed the needle into Sam's shoulder, immediately causing him to grin with a satisfying hum.

As Joe worked on Sam's ear he addressed Ethan, "I assume you're Sheriff Cole?"

Ethan sat cautiously watching the procedure. "I would prefer you call me Ethan."

"Well Ethan that was some impressive driving back there. I can't believe you had that thing going so fast with the three of you on board."

"It's easy to do the impossible when you're being chased by the devil."

"I see your point."

Finishing his work on Sam, Joe closed up his kit and cleaned up the small mess he had made in the process. As he moved back to his seat across from Ethan, he reached into a side compartment and pulled out some water and snacks. He passed them to the three passengers, who immediately began devouring the bounty.

After a few minutes of peace, Joe interrupted the meal, "Now, I have some questions for the three of you."

Sam swallowed a large bite of his granola bar and tried to suppress him narcotic inducing giggling, "We have some questions also. Like why the hell are we getting shot at and who were those assholes in the cheap suits?"

"Hold up Sam. I understand your frustrations and we'll get to that in a minute, but first I need to know what has happened in the last few days leading up to today. The more I know, the more I can tell you."

Sam tried to speak, but found it difficult now that the drug was taking its full effect, so Emily stepped in and began the story. She started from the morning Sam found Mr. Kerr's envelope and ended with the chase onto the airstrip.

Joe looked at the three of them with both respect and empathy, "I can't begin to express my sympathy over the terrible losses you have suffered today. This scenario was never supposed to happen."

Emily wiped the tears from her eyes, "Why did my mom and dad have to die?"

Joe looked at her, "It was a tragic mistake that you all became involved, but I promise that their sacrifice will not have been in vain."

Ethan sat quietly by as the story was being told. He became visibly agitated as Emily described the murder of the Shashone police force as well as the execution of Jesse. As the thought of their loss festered in his mind, Ethan became infuriated and he couldn't remain silent any longer, "I think it's about time you tell us what the hell is going on, and I don't want you to hold anything back! We deserve to know everything."

Joe looked behind him at the control panel; the flight was on time and as smooth a ride he had ever felt. He turned back towards the group, confident he would have enough time to fill them in.

"Very well Ethan, you are due an explanation." Joe took a long swig of his water then began his story, "Everything leading up to today began in 1934. As you may or may not know, Antarctica is one of the last places on earth not claimed by anyone. The brutal climate makes it nearly uninhabitable.

Over the decades since it was first explored back in the early 1800s, small groups of scientists and explorers have braved the elements to search for whatever secrets may lie at the bottom of the world.

Sometime in the early 1930s, Adolf Hitler had taken power in Germany and he focused much of his efforts on strengthening Germany's military and defenses. He had spent years dispatching men around the globe in search of treasures that would help them to gain an advantage over other countries. It was during one of these expeditions based in Antarctica that a small Nazi excavation team discovered a meteorite buried deep within the ice on the coast of the Ross Sea.

After recovering the large rock from its hibernation, they began to test their find. To their delight, these tests found that the minerals that made up the meteor were not only alien to this world, but also highly explosive. After some further testing, the scientists discovered a way to stabilize the explosive properties of the rock enough to remove samples and convert them into a fuel that could be highly effective when used as a weapon."

With their prize in tow, the Nazis left the excavation site with high hopes of the future of this discovery. Everything was running smoothly up until two days into their trip back to Berlin. That's when the battleship being used as transport for the meteor hit an iceberg and sank.

The next day, a small group of survivors were rescued by an American cruiser on its way home from a training exercise in the Falkland Islands. It was here that one of the Nazi survivors told of their find. He had been the only scientist to survive the crash and the only man outside of Berlin with knowledge of the destructive potential buried within the meteor."

Sam raised his hand, "You're telling me this whole thing is about a stupid space rock?"

Joe took a swig of his water, "I know this sounds a bit crazy, but let me finish please."

Sam slumped back into his seat. Looking around in his drug induced state, he realized Emily and Ethan were both glaring at him. "I'll shut up, Jesus."

Joe cleared his throat and continued the story, "Now where was I? Oh yes. It only took the Americans two days to recover the meteor from the wreckage of the Nazi ship. After its recovery, the meteor was shipped off to a secret location in the Midwest and the Nazi prisoners were sent to a prison complex in Hawaii, with the exception of the poor soul who knew about the meteor. He spent the next twenty years of his life relegated to solitary confinement at Alcatraz.

Irritated by what she just heard, Emily interrupted, "That doesn't sound legal."

Ethan looked over to her, "It was a different time then, hon, and we did things that were thought to be right. It's just the way it was."

"Whatever," she grunted as she slumped back down into her seat.

Following the interruption, Joe continued. "The meteor was put under years of tests by some of the greatest minds of the time. At first glance, our government was just as giddy with the discovery as Hitler was. Understanding the importance of keeping this discovery secret, only a few top officials in the government even knew about its existence. Some conspiracy theorists have even speculated that the specifications for the first Atomic Bomb originated from alien technology. If only they knew just how right they were. The meteor was the cornerstone of the research leading up to the Manhattan Project. But it was agreed that the rock itself was never to be used due to its immense power and its unstable nature."

Ethan cleared his throat, drawing Joe's attention, "If it was such a secret, then how do you know of all this?"

"I'm getting to that. Now after World War II ended, the government buried the rock deep away under its complex at Area 51 in New Mexico. Having just witnessed the destructive force of both bombs dropped on Japan, President Truman was terrified of what the meteor could do if it fell in the wrong hands. It was on his order that it was moved to New Mexico.

Thirteen years had passed without any further discussion about the meteor. In fact, after Truman left office, only a few members of the intelligence community even knew of its existence. It wasn't until the winter of '57 that our communication channels discovered chatter pertaining to the "rock", which it was sometimes referred as.

Earlier that year, the reasons for his incarceration were brought to question and subsequently the Nazi scientist was released from prison and returned to Germany. Unfortunately for our government, time and the horror of his confinement didn't cause him to forget about the discovery that precipitated his detainment all those years ago."

Ethan shook his head in disbelief, "They just let him go? Shouldn't we have had a serum we could have shot him with? Didn't we have something to maybe erase his memory?"

"You've been watching too many movies. Other than a full frontal lobotomy, there wasn't anything we could do; and after twenty years in that hell hole, those who knew about his existence had either died or retired. As with many things in our government's web of red tape and history of incompetence, he slipped through the cracks."

Sam spoke up, "So what happened after he spilled his guts?"

"Well, this is where we get closer to answering your original question, Sam. Around the same time of the prisoner's release, the CIA began to hear whispers about an organization in Europe that specialized in freelance terrorism. Their actions were rumored to have touched different societies around the globe for centuries.

This shadow organization was compromised of men from all over Europe and Asia. There was no allegiance to God or country with them, just to the cause of making money. This was done through their love of creating anarchy. To be honest, it was only dumb luck that we stumbled upon them."

"Who are they?" Ethan asked, now fully engrossed in the direction the conversation had turned.

"We don't know," Joe responded. "Like I said, we only heard rumors, nothing concrete. In the interest of giving a title to this group, the Agency nicknamed them ECHO."

Emily sat up in her seat, "Why ECHO?"

"It was just a name that someone thought up early on in the investigation, something to type on reports."

Sam snorted, "Well that's stupid."

"Not really. I have always thought it fit them. Their actions have caused ripples in every society going back centuries. It's as if their touch has echoed through time."

Joe gave a quick glance back to the controls, checking to make sure they were still on schedule. Turning back he realized that the attention span of the group was fading fast, so he'd better get to the point of the story. "Anyway, ECHO had become aware of the meteor, and it was their mission to find it and offer it up to the highest bidder. A prize of this magnitude would be priceless in the black market.

Afraid that the meteor's location was compromised, the head of the CIA put a plan in motion to relocate the rock from New Mexico to a secure military facility located deep within the Adirondack Mountains. The transport carrying the meteor, now encased in a steel bomb shell, landed in Georgia on February 5th, 1958.

The B-47 bomber carrying the package was to refuel and immediately take off for upstate New York; that's when tragedy struck the mission. As fate would have it, after taking off, the B-47 collided with an incoming F-86 just off of the Savannah coast."

Ethan interrupted the story, "I heard about this on the Discovery Channel. The B-47 was carrying a nuke of some kind and after the crash it was forced to dump it into the ocean. It took place during a training accident if I'm not mistaken."

"Exactly right sheriff, and that's what the government wanted everyone to think. Can you think of a better way to hide the truth of something than to make the world believe it was something else entirely? It ended up being a useful occurrence. Now, after the casing splashed down into the ocean, the Navy sent multiple ships into the area to guard the crash site. Everyone was under the impression that the payload lost was really a hydrogen bomb; hell, the pilots didn't know what they had in the cargo hold.

Allen Dulles, who was the head of the CIA at the time, used his power to smokescreen the entire recovery operation. Once the Navy had secured the site, all communication pertaining to the payload would be directed through his office and nowhere else, even President Nixon was left in the dark.

Not wanting to raise suspicion, Dulles made sure the Navy didn't rush with the recovery efforts. Since he knew exactly where the meteor was, no one was going to take it out from under his nose."

"So what happened with the search," Sam inquired.

"About two years after the accident, the government had no luck in locating the bomb, so they called off their search and considered the weapon lost."

Getting frustrated, Sam threw his empty water bottle to the ground, "I still don't understand what this has to do with us!"

"Okay lad, just calm down. I'm getting to that." Joe checked the cockpit once more, everything remained on schedule. Turning back, he continued, "Now fast-forward sixteen years. It's 1976, and I was a rookie agent with the CIA. My first assignment was to join a veteran in Moscow to help gather all the intel we could on the Soviets and its leader Leonid Brezhnev. I would end up spending the next fourteen years of my life with my new partner and friend, Gerald Simmons. You kids might know him as Jerry, or Mr. Kerr."

Joe paused a minute to let that bit of information sink in. The kids both turned towards each other and mouthed the same curse word that began with an "f".

"Gerald and I quickly formed a bond built on trust and mutual respect. He saved my life a few times, and I would return the favor on more than one occasion. After the Berlin Wall came down and the Cold War had ended, there was no one left to fight, so Gerald decided to retire. It was during our last drunken night in Berlin that he told me the story of Bend, Oregon. In 1963, he had been tasked with watching a former government agent who had disappeared a few years prior. During his surveillance, Gerald witnessed the agent's brutal slaying. After Gerald dispatched the assailants, he rushed over to the dying man. Before he took his last breath, the man handed over what now lies in the box sitting right over there." Joe points down below Sam's chair at Mr. Kerr's lockbox.

"Within that box is the only map with the hidden location of the lost meteor. Even though Gerald was able to uncover the history surrounding the meteor, the only surviving person with the story of how it was located and moved from the bottom of the ocean died in 1963. What I do know is that those men chasing you are some of the new order of ECHO. They have never given up hope on finding the meteor, and it looks like they are as determined as ever."

Ethan leaned forward, "Why did Mr. Kerr, I mean Agent Simmons, move to Shashone Peak?"

"Well he was from Wyoming originally. Gerald was born and raised in Cheyenne. He figured that no one knew that territory like he did, and seeing that Shashone Peak is just a small blip on the map, it was the perfect place to disappear.

After he had settled in, I received a letter from him; it was coded so that only I knew its contents. In the letter he informed me of his location and after some further correspondence, we had set up this failsafe in case anything happened to him."

The cabin fell silent for a few moments before Emily spoke up, "So what are we going to do now?"

Joe looked at his watch, "We have another couple of hours of flight time until we reach Wisconsin."

"What's in Wisconsin," Sam asked.

"That's where were going to land and stash this plane. From there we need to make our way to my place in

Chicago. Once in Chicago, we need to get you kids to safety. You have already suffered enough for ten lifetimes, there's no point in putting you through anymore."

Standing, Sam looked over at Emily, then back to Joe, "We have just lost everything important to us. Everyone we knew is dead and our home was burned to the ground. We're not going anywhere until this is finished." Defiant in his statement, Sam sat back down, never taking his eyes off of Joe.

Joe looked to Ethan for help. He just shrugged off the glance, "Don't look at me man. I wouldn't want to be the one standing in their way."

Shaking his head in frustration, Joe stood and looked down at the three passengers, "Get some rest. We'll discuss this after we land."

Making his way back into the cockpit, Joe resumed his position behind the wheel of the Cessna. In the dimly lit cabin, Emily, Ethan and Sam all drifted away into a well-deserved slumber as the first light of a new day began to glow off in the distance.

Chapter

Nine

July 30th

8:35am

The Drake Hotel

Chicago, Illinois

The sound of shoes scuffing along the floor echoed through the peaceful hotel room as the morning sun arose on another day. In the master bedroom of the exotic suite, a groggy figure was awakened from his vodka-induced hibernation.

As he sat up in the plush king sized bed, his sluggish gaze lazily scanned the suite for the source of the disturbance. In the adjacent sitting room of the suite, a middle-aged woman dressed in a light blue maid's uniform was straightening up. She was humming away to the music pumping into her ears from the small mp3 player tucked beneath her apron.

Retrieving the new linens she brought for the bed, she looked into the open bedroom door. Upon noticing the man staring at her, the maid gasped and lowered her head as she pulled the car buds out and stuffed them into her pocket. "Please, I am so sorry. I knocked but there was no answer, and you didn't have the Do Not Disturb sign out," she pleaded, her voice trembling.

Stretching the man pulled back the covers exposing his tanned, muscular physique. He was a bronze statue, strong and flawless. His long auburn hair draped down his back; the strands of grey peppered throughout now shinning in the morning sun. As he stood, the woman froze in place; her body trembling in shock over his lack of clothing.

He was not shy about his exposed body; in fact he strutted with a confident swagger. Stopping in front of the frightened woman, the man slowly scanned her body, "Why are you shaking my dear? Is this any way to treat a guest of your beautiful hotel?"

"I…I'm sorry sir. I should have checked if anyone was here. I'll just leave and give you some privacy."

As she turned, he grabbed her arm and pulled her ear close to his mouth. "I don't remember dismissing you," he said as he reached out and began to caress her cheek, her soft skin moist from fresh tears.

A quiet buzzing emanating from the computer in the main room of the suite interrupted the now tense situation. "Excuse me my dear; work beckons." The man placed a soft kiss on the trembling woman's forehead, and then released her. Turning his backside to her, he walked over to the computer.

He grinned as the door to the room slammed shut behind him; another satisfied customer.

The computer buzzed to life with different encryption sequences loading. After patiently waiting a second for the program to boot up, he sat in the leather desk chair and entered his thirteen digit code, connecting him to the incoming message. The screen changed over to a video feed of a small figure hidden by shadows.

"*Are you alone*," an electronically distorted voice inquired from the other end.

"I am."

"It's good to see you're still alive Sabre. Now can you please explain to me why your team is wasting our time and money when the package is still at large?!"

Sabre was taken aback by his employer's sudden rise in tone, "Excuse me, but you do not ever address me in that manner. I have sacrificed much in the pursuit of your little trinket and I deserve some respect."

"Enough of your posturing Sabre, we are not impressed by your incompetence."

Sabre fell silent as the shock of his employer's audacity paralyzed him.

"We will not tolerate excuses. This organization has sought after this prize for decades, and we have never been closer to revealing its true location. Now, I have read your report and find the fact that they disappeared into thin air hard to believe. Can you explain?"

Still shell shocked by the conversation, Sabre cleared his throat, "Whoever picked them up was connected. After the plane landed in Wisconsin, they drove into Chicago and just vanished."

The line remained silent.

"So after the trail went cold I decided to take a night to regroup before continuing the hunt."

"*We will tell you when it's time to rest. Until then, you will continue with your assignment. Now can you take care of this small task alone, or do you need help handling these children?*"

Slowly standing, his hands clenched into fists, Sabre leaned into the microphone on the laptop, "It will be done ma'am."

With a sudden swiping motion, he sent the computer crashing against the wall to his left. The remaining pixels of the screen flickered than disappeared behind a wall of darkness. Sabre remained standing, his exposed backside facing the morning sun. The veins in his neck pulsed with a seething hatred for those who he took orders from. The effect of his recent conversation boiling over caused him to let out a roar of frustration.

His loud cry sent an echo throughout the top floor of the building, sending his man in the adjacent room into a panicked frenzy.

The front door exploded open as Holger barreled his way in, his pistol raised in preparation of whatever he might find.

To Sabre's chagrin, Holger was naked, except for a pair of silk boxer shorts covered in pictures of *Sponge Bob Square Pants*.

"Are you alright sir?! I heard shout."

Noticing that Sabre was fully exposed, Holger shaded his eyes in embarrassment. Sabre took a deep breath and relaxed his clenched torso.

Looking over to the large man standing in his doorway, he just shook his head in disgust, "Have you ever heard of knocking, you dolt?!"

Still hiding his eyes, Holger apologized for his entrance, "I'm sorry sir. I hear scream and thought you might have trouble."

"The only trouble I have is that my men are all three-hundred pound, ignorant children."

Sabre walked into his bedroom and recovered the plush terrycloth robe hastily thrown on the leather recliner in the corner of the room. He approached Holger as he cinched up the belt, "I have just been informed that we have rested enough. Go wake up the others, it's time to get back to work."

"Yes sir," Holger shouted as he turned and quickly exited the uncomfortable situation.

Sabre turned back to the desk where his former laptop had rested. Retrieving a small leather billfold from the desktop, he opened it as he rubbed his left temple. The situation had forced him to change tactics, and he began to feel a sense of nostalgia over the loss of one of his favorite aliases. He had used the persona of Special Agent Johnson many times in his past, but now the ID had been compromised. Normally those who discovered his ruse never lived long enough to cause him to precipitate a change; but the current developments had forced his hand.

"Goodbye old friend," he uttered as he threw the badge into the fireplace. As it burned away to nothing, Sabre pondered his next move. It was time to find that which eluded him.

Chapter

Ten

Joliet, Illinois
July 31st, 2013
10:45am

It had been a few days since the small Cessna had reached
its destination and so far, no sign of ECHO. In an attempt
to avoid detection, Joe had landed at Rutherford Airport in
Arkansaw, Wisconsin. It was a privately owned airport, and
the manager owed him a favor. After landing, the group
helped hide the plane in an old hanger located at the rear of
the airfield.

Borrowing a van, they then made their way into Joliet, a city just southwest of Chicago, Illinois. It was here that they found sanctuary.

Back in the mid-nineties, Joe had purchased an abandoned warehouse for emergency situations just like the one he now faced. It was on the outskirts of town, perfect for disappearing.

This remote location had one entrance from a small dirt road, and the building was surrounded by a dense tree line. The rear of the building was about three hundred feet from a set of seldom-used railroad tracks.

Within the complex where his property was located was a few other abandoned buildings that were in disrepair. The entire location was an eyesore, and the people of the area had chosen to forget about it. After investing some time and funds into the property, Joe had built a solid base of operations.

He had spent the morning sitting at a small kitchen table sipping many steaming cups of coffee. The morning sun was beginning to shine through the open window adjacent to the table. His breakfast of toast and eggs sat half eaten as he looked out the window, lost in thought.

"How're the eggs in this dump," Ethan said as he entered the room. He was clean for the first time in days, and surprisingly well rested. Joe had given him a pair of jeans and an old Chicago Bears t-shirt. Per Joe's request, Ethan had shaved off his mustache and clipped his hair into a short buzz cut.

Joe looked down at his plate, "A little dry but they're better than nothing."

Ethan walked over to the counter and poured himself a large cup of coffee. He turned back towards Joe and leaned on the counter, "So, what now chief?"

Looking around, Joe seemed to be searching for something, "Where are the kids?"

"They're still in bed. I didn't want to wake them, they need the rest."

"That they do. They've shown exceptional bravery; you all have."

"Yeah well it didn't help save any of my men. Speaking of which, I need to get back home as soon as possible. Do you have any information about the condition of the town?"

Joe sat up in the chair and nervously looked at his hands, "I don't think you're going back there anytime soon Ethan."

"What the hell are you talking about?"

"I received word last night that your town has been wiped from the map. The fire spread quickly without any first responders to help contain the situation, and it eventually burned to the ground. You and the kids are feared dead along with most of the residents of Shoshone Peak. Those who survived were silenced."

"WHAT!! How do you destroy a whole town?"

"ECHO has always excelled at covering their tracks. They have members in most state and local governments around the world and it only took a few phone calls to come up with a natural event that would be believed. In the end, the destruction was blamed on a freak wild fire due to a lightning strike. This time of year a scenario like that is plausible. I am sorry Ethan."

Dropping his coffee mug to the ground, Ethan rested his face in his hands; the pain of what he just heard was overwhelming. As the terrible revelation was being told, both men were unaware of Sam and Emily standing in the doorway.

"When were you going to tell us," Sam asked, catching both men by surprise.

Joe jumped to his feet, "Sam. Emily. How long have you been listening?"

Emily, now numb to the terrible events that had occurred, walked up to Joe and looked him in his eyes, "My brother asked you a question."

"I know he did; please, sit, join us," Joe motioned for the kids to sit at the table.

Sam and Emily sat down, both looking rested. Emily had her hair in a ponytail; she wore a new pair of jeans and a hooded sweatshirt from the local K-Mart; a light blue one with dolphins decorating the front. Her beautiful young face now showed the wear of someone twice her age.

Sam had on a pair of khaki cargo shorts and he was also wearing a Bears t-shirt; he was lucky to get the blue one. His left arm was pulled against his chest, tucked away in a new sling Joe was able to score from a friend who worked at Silver Cross Hospital. His right ear was bandaged; the bleeding from his missing piece had finally stopped, but just in case it started again they wrapped it back up tight.

Joe addressed the group, "Our main objective now is to protect you kids. Even though we may have lost ECHO, I guarantee they're still looking for the box and eventually they will track us down. I think the best course of action will be to split up. With Gerald gone, the box is now my burden. I will take it and disappear after I figure out what to do with you three. I still have some contacts in the Bureau and it shouldn't be that hard to get you relocated to somewhere safe. Unfortunately you will all have to leave everything behind and change your identities."

Sam quickly protested, cutting off his sister before she could speak, "I'm not going to sit on my ass while my town and family burn. That damn box is my responsibility and I will decide what happens to it!"

Emily slapped his arm, causing him to wince, "You mean our responsibility, don't you."

Joe rocked himself out of the chair and onto his feet. He walked over and stepped in between the siblings, "Would you please keep your damn voices down. We need to remain in control. Now, this is not up for debate. You kids are not strong enough to fight these men. You cannot imagine the power they possess."

"Bullshit," Sam snapped back, "We have just as much of a right to come along as anyone."

"Yeah," Emily added defiantly.

Trying to remain calm, Joe lowered his voice to a softer tone, "I feel awful for your loss, but I'm not going to drag two teenagers along with me. This is going to be dangerous, and I only need help from those who have the training to be useful. Now that's the end of the discussion!"

"This is total crap," Sam snorted in anger. "Are you just gonna sit there sheriff, or are you planning on helping?"

Ethan chose to remain quiet as the battle had begun. He was still reeling from the revelation that the town didn't exist anymore.

"Sheriff," Sam screamed at the top of his lungs.

"For the last time, I am not the goddamn sheriff anymore," Ethan yelled as he reached out and grabbed Sam's shirt, no longer able to control his growing rage. "There's nothing left of our town. We are on the run from a group of terrorists and it is a miracle that we're still alive. You need to get this through your thick skull!"

As Sam recoiled in shock he instinctively threw a punch at Ethan in defense. Luckily his hand came up just short, brushing against Ethan's chin. Joe quickly scooped up Sam in a bear hug and tried his best to subdue the large boy.

In defense of her brother, Emily grabbed a knife off of the table and placed the blade in the small of Joe's back, "Let him go," she commanded.

Returning himself to a state of calm, Ethan tried to reason with the terrified young woman, "Emily, put the knife down."

Emily remained eerily calm as she kept the pressure of the blade against Joe's back. As Ethan inched closer, her gaze focused on him.

"Stop or I'll cut him. Don't screw with me Ethan."

Heeding her threat, he stopped dead in his tracks. The group found themselves in a stalemate.

"Alright everyone, let's just calm down," Joe requested as he lightened his grip on Sam.

Sam tore himself from Joe's grasp and spun to face him, "Just because we're not spies doesn't mean that we can't kick some ass."

Emily lowered the knife but she never moved her steely gaze from Joe.

Joe and Sam stared each other down for a few minutes before they were interrupted by a knock at the front door.

"Are we expecting pizza?" Ethan questioned, alarmed by the unexpected visitor.

Joe looked around the room for a waepon, "There are only two people in the world that know of this place and one is dead. You need to find a place to hide, now!"

The group scattered as Joe removed a Franchi 720 semi-automatic shotgun from under the kitchen table. After pumping a shell into the chamber, he moved swiftly to the door.

The LCD screen glowing just left of the door was linked to a security camera located outside above the entrance. The state-of-the-art system was focused on a dark figure standing on the other side of the door. This person was aware of the surveillance and did his best to keep his identity hidden from the camera. He wore a long, black trench coat and a baseball cap.

"You have exactly five seconds to identify yourself before I tear you in half," Joe threatened as he placed the barrel of his gun against the door. The power from this twenty gauge monster could easily rip right through the door and anything or anyone on the other side.

The figure removed his hat and slowly raised his head.

"It can't be," Joe mumbled in utter disbelief. Lowering his weapon, Joe reached for the digital keypad on the door and entered the ten digit pass-code. As the lock clicked, Joe grabbed the door handle and pulled it open. The man standing on the other side smiled at his host.

"How're tricks Joe," the man asked as he offered his hand.

Still in shock, Joe reached up and accepted the man's hand, shaking it vigorously, "Oh, you know Gerald, just another day in paradise."

ᕫ

The group watched in silence as Gerald devoured a plate of bacon and eggs. He was visibly exhausted from his travels, but the kids were amazed at how spry the once frail man still seemed.

Gerald finished off his meal then took a large swig of coffee. As he sat back in his chair, he let out a long sigh of relief. "That was just what I needed," he said as he rubbed his now full belly.

"You still have an appetite like a hog," Joe said as he stood and cleared the dirty plates. He brought them over to the sink and began to clean up. He figured that there were questions the others might have and he didn't want to be anywhere near the tidal wave that was about to crash down around Gerald.

"What happened with you," Sam asked, breaking the silence.

Gerald wiped his mouth with his napkin and took another sip of his coffee. Clearing his throat he addressed the young man, "That's a long story my boy."

"Well we aint going anywhere 'til you spill it, so please enlighten us," Ethan interjected. Sam, Emily and Ethan all sat watching the old man, eagerly awaiting his answer.

"I guess you deserve the truth."

"Uhh, ya think," Emily added sarcastically.

Gerald reached out to grab her hand, but she pulled away in disgust. She blamed the man for everything that had happened, and whatever answer he gave wouldn't be enough for her to forgive him.

Ashamed by his weak gesture, Gerald pulled his hand back, "I had lived in Shashone Peak for over twenty years without anything happening. It was my goal to remain a hermit and I had hoped that the world would forget about the meteorite."

Sam was confused by this, "Don't you mean ECHO? Who else knew about it?"

"A small faction of our government still knew. They might have not known its whereabouts, but they knew it still existed."

Ethan raised his hand as if he was still in school, "Why does that matter? Didn't they just want to hide it?"

"Come on sheriff, you're smarter than that."

Ethan's face began to turn red as he had reached his boiling point over constantly being referred to as sheriff. Looking to prevent a fight, Joe immediately interjected, "It would be best if you called him Ethan from now on. Trust me."

"Whatever floats your boat." Gerald took another sip of coffee, cleared his throat and continued, "Anyway, Ethan, in the mid-1950s the Korean War had just ended. With that conflict over, our government quickly became concerned with the rising threat growing in Russia, and it was decided that we needed to harness the power of the meteor to create a first strike weapon.

The secret installation in the Adirondack Mountains was actually a secured weapons development site focused on the research and development of WMD's. It was after finding this out that a small group from within our government decided to locate and hide the meteor. They knew that the use of this destructive force could drastically change the course of human existence."

The group remained in a stunned silence after this news. Emily was the first to question what they just heard,

"How did they get the meteor without the government knowing?"

"Well now that's the million dollar question. After I was thrust into this role, my knowledge of what occurred after the crash consisted of everything I have just told you. How they did it has been lost to history."

Joe grabbed the coffee pot and refilled Gerald's mug, "So where ya been hiding?"

"I'm getting to that. Now after the Fourth of July celebration this month, I felt an uncomfortable vibe in town. It didn't take me long to realize I was being watched. Over the next few weeks, my home was under surveillance, and I had gained a tail during my daily walks. The night before I left the note on your doorstep, my house was broken into. The perpetrators fled after I confronted them with my AR-15, but I had a feeling that it wasn't a simple burglary. That night I hid the box and quickly typed up the letter."

"Why us," Sam questioned.

"I needed a place that I thought they wouldn't look, and all I could picture was the two of you sitting on that porch playing games. I thought that you would be able to go unnoticed."

Getting irritated, Emily butted in on the conversation, "Well obviously they followed you to our house when you dropped off the letter. How else would they know about us?"

"That's the part I couldn't get my head around at first. I didn't go to your house that night. After leaving my house I went to Rusty's Tavern on Main Street and asked Ed Taylor to drop it off in the morning when he delivered your paper. After giving him a hundred dollar bill, I hoped that he would keep it secret."

"Well he obviously told someone," Ethan interjected.

Gerald wiped his face and looked at the group; his eyes were now red with tears. "I returned to what was left of the town before coming here, and he was nowhere to be found. Who knows what information they got out of him, but I would bet that tough old bastard put up quite a fight. Either way he's probably dead because of me. A lot of people are."

Sam jumped to his feet, "Don't forget about our parents you son of a bitch!"

Gerald raised his hands in an attempt to calm Sam, "I never meant for this to happen Sam. I had hoped that by running, ECHO would follow me and leave you all in peace."

Ethan rose from his chair, standing next to Sam who still shook with anger, "Well that didn't work out so well for the town, did it?"

Sam lunged for Gerald but he was caught in midair by Ethan's strong hands. Gerald sat motionless as the boy fought against Ethan's grip, waiting to receive whatever punishment that was coming. He knew he deserved to answer for every ounce of pain and suffering these kids had endured.

Growing increasingly frustrated by the altercation, Emily stepped between the two men and grabbed her brother by the face, "Sam, enough!"

The touch of his sister's hands calmed Sam enough so that Ethan could release him. Emily stood between Sam and Gerald, her hands now cradling his face. She smiled at him as tears flowed down both of their cheeks. "I know Mr. Kerr has caused us pain, and he will have to answer to us eventually; but right now he is the only man who can help us and I can't lose you like I lost mom and dad."

Her words calmed his rage. Sam stared into her eyes and felt the same warmth and love he had always received from his mom when he was sad. Exhausted from the deluge of emotions he now felt, Sam collapsed into Emily's arms and began to sob. As she comforted her brother, Emily turned to look at Gerald.

"You are the one who caused this pain, and you better figure out a way to fix it."

Her threat hung in the air as she led Sam out of the kitchen. Ethan looked at both Joe and Gerald then he drained the rest of his coffee in one big gulp.

"Don't think I'm on your side. My town burned because of this mess and I want my pound of flesh. You just have to decide if it's going to come from you or the other bad guys."

He slammed his empty cup down on the table to punctuate his final remark. Turning in disgust, Ethan followed the kids into the living room, leaving the two stunned men behind.

Joe walked over to the table and sat down in the chair across from his friend.

Gerald looked at Joe with tears still welling in his eyes, "What else could I have done?"

"Listen man, I know you made the only choice you could. We both know that these things don't always work out, and there's always some collateral damage."

"What should I do Joe? How can I ever make this right?"

Picking up Ethan's empty coffee cup, Joe's voice became filled an intense ferocity, "The only way we know how. We need to find ECHO and take them out once and for all." As the final word left his lips, Joe threw Ethan's empty cup across the room. As the glass shattered against the wall, a small fire began to grow in the hearts of the two spies. It was time to go to war.

Chapter
Eleven

Chicago, Illinois
1:37pm

Doctor Henry Ryan lay bloodied and dying on the floor of his luxury apartment near downtown Chicago.

Earlier that day two police officers had approached him at his work place. He was the current director of Silver Cross Hospital in Joliet, and also one of its top cardiologists. After a brief discussion in which the men grilled him about a couple of fugitives who may have received medical care at the hospital, Henry had been encouraged by the officers to come with them to the local precinct.

Being an intelligent man, it didn't take Henry long to realize the deception, and he chose to leave with them in the hope of keeping hospital staff and patients from harm.

Henry was a former Navy Corpsman, and he had experience dealing with interrogation. He had spent a summer in a Vietnamese prison facility in the northern province of Son La and he had endured several horrible beatings, but he never broke.

Upon arriving at his apartment, the men had beat Henry with everything and anything that they could find.

He had endured hours of brutal torture before he finally snapped. It was under the intense scrutiny that he divulged the name of his oldest and dearest friend, Joe Pagano.

As he gasped for his last breath, one of his abductors kicked Henry in the head for good measure. The satisfying crunch was music to his ears.

"He was a tough old man, I'll give him that," Sabre exclaimed as he cracked his bloodied knuckles, a satisfying grin now growing across his face.

Holger was in the other room changing out of his blood-covered police uniform, when his cell phone buzzed in his jacket.

"What news," he asked the caller. The answer sent him sprinting into the other room, "Sir, we may have them."

"Good, now clean up this mess. We need to make it look like a home invasion," Sabre instructed as he accepted the phone.

Holger reluctantly shook his head in acknowledgement and went about the grisly task.

"This is Sabre. Please tell me some good news, Franc."

"Yes sir, I think I may have found our pilot. There is a small abandoned warehouse not far from the hospital where we took the doctor. Something is not right about this place."

"I need more evidence you idiot, not just your hunch."

"I understand sir. Anton and I have already tasked one of our satellites to take thermal images of the building. The warehouse is not part of the local power grid, but there is a heavy trace of electrical interference. It seems to be powered by multiple generators."

Sabre sat down on the doctor's very nice Saddler leather sofa. Pondering over what he just heard, Sabre decided to make a move.

"I want you and Anton to set up surveillance around the site and keep me posted about any movement. Holger and I will join you shortly. Do nothing until I arrive, do you understand?"

"*Yes sir!*"

Sabre ended the call. He had been unlucky so far, but it seemed the tables may have finally been turned. Jumping into action, he sprinted to the bedroom where his pressed Armani suit lay in wait. As he began to change from his police uniform, Sabre's mind raced with every scenario he could think of.

"Holger," he shouted, beckoning to his man in the other room.

The large German poked his head into the room, "Yes sir!"

"I need you to finish that up. We leave in five."

"Yes sir," the large man shouted as he hurriedly returned to his task.

Sabre changed as fast as he could while trying to remain calm and focused. A nervous energy flowed through his fingers making it difficult to cope with tying his tie. For today he would not only catch those who had evaded him, he would also finally silence his critics back home. Today, he was God.

⌒

Joe had spent the afternoon brainstorming with Gerald and Ethan over the best course of action. That morning he had seen a disturbing alert on television pertaining to a terrorist attack at Rutherford Airport. The initial report explained the condition of the owner and his ground crew. Their bodies were badly burned and each suffered multiple breaks before they had been incinerated. It appeared as if they were tortured.

After passing along this story to Gerald and Ethan, they had all agreed that it would only be a matter of time before ECHO would locate the warehouse, and it was imperative that they moved from this location.

Joe pressed the issue that if they were to survive, Sam and Emily would also have to flee the country and disappear; it was the only way. The siblings fought the decision at first, but it didn't take long before Gerald and Joe had them convinced there wasn't another option.

Ethan had volunteered to stay with the kids, becoming their guardian for the time being. With his family and friends all gone he had nothing to keep him here, and over their travels he had become close to the kids.

Joe was to travel with them and help with the relocation. He had some friends left in the Netherlands and he knew better than anyone how to vanish. Once they left the warehouse they would travel light and fast. He would lead the group to Brunswick Golden Isles Airport in Brunswick, Georgia. Ten years ago, one of Joe's former partners moved to Georgia and set up a flying school in Brunswick. He would be able to offer temporary shelter and transportation to Europe. It was the least he could do for an old friend who once saved his life.

Gerald's path would take him north into Canada. He had a small cabin in the Canadian Yukon that he had built many years ago. He would travel to the location and spend the rest of his days watching over the lockbox and the secrets that lay within it. His fate was forever tied to its contents.

As they finalized the details, Sam was packing up some clothes and supplies that Joe had stashed for a rainy day. Other than some spare clothes, he also stuffed away a small dome tent, two flashlights with spare batteries, four packs of water proof matches, three hundred dollars in small bills and finally a small Bowie knife, just in case of any surprise visitors. Joe had informed him of their travel plans and with it, the likelihood of sleeping in the wild.

Hotels have too many cameras and attract too much attention.

As Sam finished securing his bag, he began to hum the theme song to The A-Team; it was his Dad's favorite show and one that they would watch together anytime they came across a rerun.

"I miss them too," Emily interrupted as she walked into the room.

Sam turned suddenly, "Christ Em, you scared the crap out of me."

"Mr. Kerr told me that being jumpy is good. It means were focused."

"I don't think we need to call him Mr. Kerr anymore. The bastard has a name."

Emily walked over and leaned against the desk next to the bed, "It's not his fault, Sam."

"How can you say that? If it wasn't for him, Mom and Dad would still be alive." Sam slammed his pack on the floor and sat down in its place. He removed the knife from its home in his pack and stared at it. "I've thought about sticking it into his eye, just so he could feel the pain our parents had to deal with."

Shocked by his sudden violent tone, Emily reached her hand towards Sam, "How about you give that to me before you hurt yourself?"

Sam remained focused on the blade as he turned it in his hands. "I wonder how many innocent people have died because of him and that stupid box."

Emily continued to hold her hand out, "You're blaming the wrong people. I'm not saying Gerald is not to blame for anything. I just think you need to focus on the true villains, ECHO. Now please give me the knife."

Sam looked up at Emily and stared coldly into her eyes. He jumped from the bed, causing Emily to stumble back onto the desk. He reached out with his free hand and caught her now trembling arm. As he pulled her back up, Sam slapped the knife into her still outstretched hand. "Take it."

Releasing her, he turned and left the room. Emily remained behind, shocked by what had just happened. She realized that the events of the previous week may have changed her brother into something she didn't recognize. She just hoped that someday they both would be normal again.

ᔕ

"Team two, what is your status?"

"*We are on the west end of compound sir. The exit has been covered.*"

"Excellent. Keep your wits about you gentlemen. We cannot let them get away this time."

"*Yes sir.*"

The radio crackled then went silent. Sabre had parked his vehicle just south of the warehouse before making his way to a silo on the southern portion of the complex. His location was elevated enough to give him a birds-eye view of the entire location.

After losing a few men in Wyoming, Sabre had to be creative when planning his assault on the warehouse. He knew that at least two of the men inside were armed and well trained. He didn't fear the children, but after their heroics during their first encounter, he knew not to underestimate them.

Including him, the team had been broken down into two two-man fire teams and two one-man scout teams. Tau and Franc had taken a few light machine guns and dug themselves in just inside the tree line north of the main building.

Holger and Amun were positioned at the entrance to the compound. Sabre had acquired a military grade Humvee equipped with a 50 caliber machine gun attached to the roof of the vehicle. The truck was far enough in from the main road to not attract attention, and the barrel of the gun was faced directly at the mass of buildings.

Anton was stationed in a tree next to the railroad tracks. He was perched forty feet up with his trusty Dragunov SVD sniper rifle. This weapon had been a gift from his mother after he was accepted into Russian Special Forces or "Spetsnaz". He had seventy-three confirmed kills during his time in the service, but he had estimated at least fifty to sixty more were unconfirmed. It was his excellent marksmanship that first attracted ECHO to him six years prior.

Sabre had quickly found his perch on top of the thirty-five foot red silo. He would begin the fight lying in the prone position with a pair of binoculars and his own purveyor of death and destruction. Sabre was not a subtle man and he wanted to make a statement, so he had located a RPG-7V antitank launcher equipped with an OG-7V antipersonnel round plus a few TBG-7V thermobaric rounds, just in case they needed to show their adversary a glimpse of hell. This little monster cost a few bucks, but it would guarantee him the effect he desired. Each OG-7V would work to cause death and destruction, but the thermobaric warheads would destroy everything and anything in its path.

It had been twenty-minutes since they had become settled into their positions and the team was becoming antsy. Lucky for them, they would not have to wait long.

After one last gear check, Joe readied the group for their departure. Sam and Emily now wore jeans and matching University of Chicago t-shirts and hats. Ethan had changed into khakis and a button down shirt. They were going to make the attempt to disguise themselves as a family out on vacation visiting colleges.

It had been a few days since the initial attack and Sam's shoulder was only about fifty percent, but it was good enough to where he didn't need the sling anymore. That would be one less thing to help draw attention to the group. He had tilted his hat sideways so that the bill covered what was left of his ear. It wasn't a perfect disguise, but it was the best they could do on such short notice.

Joe was decked out in jeans, a t-shirt and a tattered leather jacket. The day before he had "borrowed" a cab from McNamara Cab Company and changed the plate numbers. It was his intention to act as a simple cab driver taking the family around town. He had hoped the ruse would get them out of Illinois without drawing any unwanted attention, but in case they were found out, the trunk held a small arsenal. After they had cleared Illinois, they would ditch the vehicle and acquire less conspicuous transportation east.

Gerald was a little less discreet. He was in full camouflage and he carried a large pack on his back. He had a shoulder holster with a fully loaded Desert Eagle ready for action. The pack contained the lockbox and enough provisions to sustain him on his long journey north into Canada. Joe had an old BMW R100RS motorcycle that he had restored, and Gerald was eager to open up the old beauty on his trip.

Finally, it was time to move and everyone mustered at the door. As they stowed their gear, Gerald put a hand on Emily and Sam's shoulder. "I can never apologize enough for your loss. When I had met you both, you were barely out of diapers and because of recent events you have become strong, resilient adults. I know your parents would be very proud of you."

Emily smiled at the old man, but Sam wasn't as forgiving. He slapped away Gerald's hand and stepped nose-to-nose with the spy. "Don't think that you're off the hook with me. You're as much to blame as ECHO." He turned his back to Gerald and readjusted his pack.

"Don't mind him," Emily said, "He'll get over it in time. He's just stubborn." To his surprise, she embraced the old man. "Good luck, and please be safe."

"Thank you, my dear. You watch after Sam now. He'll need you."

Gerald stepped away from Emily and turned towards Joe and Ethan, who were busy making one last check of the gear. It was obvious that Sam's words still cut very deep. "Please keep them safe gentlemen. I've caused them so much anguish; they deserve some peace."

Joe embraced his friend. "Don't be concerned with us. Ethan and I will get them away from all of this madness. I only hope you will arrive at your destination in one piece. I will contact you when we have arrived in Middleburg."

The old friends stepped out of their bear hug and shook hands, both aware of the fact that this might be the last time they see each other.

Gerald turned his attention to Ethan, who was impatiently watching as everyone said their goodbyes.

"I am sorry for everything Ethan. I know how much that town meant to you. I only hope that you can forgive me." Gerald extended his right hand as a gesture of friendship, but it would remain empty. Ethan stood with his arms folded and glared at Gerald, "That town was everything to me, it was my whole world. Earlier this week I had to watch it burn. I have watched my friends get slaughtered like animals and all this over a piece of paper you carry on your back."

Ethan stepped closer to Gerald, "You need to make it out of here or all of our sacrifices have been for squat. So you better not screw this up."

"I won't let you down, any of you."

Ethan turned his back on Gerald and picked up his back pack. After flipping the pack onto his back he reached for the door, "Good, because I don't want this happening to anyone else, even the Canadians."

There was a small chuckle from the group as Ethan slid open the door. The laughter would be silenced by the crack from a rifle. Ethan's left shoulder exploded into a red cloud as his body was thrown back. He collapsed to the floor at Emily's feet. She began to scream as blood squirted out of the wound. Thinking quickly, Sam jumped for the door and slid it shut just as two rounds buried themselves deep into the heavily reinforced metal.

Joe rushed to Ethan's aide, applying pressure to the now seeping wound. Gerald joined Sam in securing the door. Expecting an army to break through the door, the group was surprised that nothing followed the initial shots. Joe continued to hold pressure on Ethan's shoulder.

"Emily," he shouted to the still screaming girl. She stopped and looked at Joe, wide-eyed with terror. "I need you to go into the bathroom and bring me the red bag with a white cross on it. Can you do that for me?" She remained silent but shook her head vigorously in acknowledgement. "Good, now go, fast!"

Snapping out of her shock, Emily sprinted towards the bathroom.

Ethan writhed on the ground in agony, his clothes now saturated with blood.

"Sam I need your help," Joe called to the boy.

Gerald slapped Sam on the arm, "Go lad, the door's secure."

Sam left Gerald at the door and hustled to Joe's side.

"I need you to hold him down if you can," Joe instructed as Emily returned with the bag.

Sam grabbed Ethan's legs and fought to keep them still. "Thank you Emily, now I need you to hold Ethan's right arm down as I try to stop the bleeding."

Emily did as she was told, the entire time fighting back the urge to vomit.

"Ahhhh," Ethan screamed as Joe ripped open his shirt, exposing the wound.

"Now Ethan, I need you try and remain still. The round passed clean through, but I don't want to use morphine because we need you to be sharp. So when I fix you up, it's gonna hurt like a son of a bitch."

"Just friggin do it already," Ethan snapped as he continued to grimace in pain.

Joe first retrieved a packet of *Wounded Warrior* from his bag. This packet contained a granular coagulant that is used to stop bleeding during combat situations. He poured the entire packet into the wound, causing Ethan to scream in agony. After the substance began to slow the bleeding, Joe removed a field dressing from the pack. He wrapped Ethan's shoulder tight and secured the bandage with a roll of gauze.

Once the bleeding had stopped and Ethan was stabilized, Joe sat back with a temporary sigh of relief. "I need you both to stay with Ethan," he said as he looked at the terrified kids.

"We're not going anywhere," Sam said as he let go of Ethan's legs. After the initial shock of the treatment, Ethan had stopped squirming as he began to grow accustomed to the pain. Sam scooted down to where Emily still held onto Ethan's arm. He wrapped his good arm around her shoulder and held her as they both watched over their wounded friend.

Joe moved swiftly over to the door where Gerald stood watch.

"How the hell did they find us?" Gerald asked, slightly irritated.

"They found you before, didn't they," Joe shouted over the sound of the incoming gunfire.

"Good point."

Joe sprinted over to his computer; it was here where images from all of his cameras converged. He had spent quite a bit of time hiding multiple cameras throughout the property. Most were hidden within tree branches, almost undetectable.

He fired up the monitor and focused his attention on the images now flashing before his eyes. There were ten cameras but only four were still transmitting images. Whoever was out there must have a way to disrupt the cameras electrical signatures. As he panned the remaining cameras, he could make out the south and east of the compound, but little else. As he watched the screen for any sign of life, camera two picked up the form of a man. Adjacent to the railroad tracks, a large man could be seen perched up a tree. His awkward position gave away more than just his location; it also made it hard for the man to completely hide the large rifle he was holding.

"Gerald, come here a sec," Joe shouted.

Gerald darted over to the monitor, "What do you see?"

"They have taken out most of the cameras, but this one picked up something. What do you make of this?"

"I'll be damned. That looks like a Dragunov. I bet he's the son-of-a-bitch who clipped Ethan."

"Well I have a little surprise for him." Joe typed a few lines of code into his computer and a targeting reticle appeared over the man's image. Joe moved the crosshairs a little to the left, aligning them perfectly over the assassin's entire frame.

As he worked, Ethan, Sam and Emily joined the men at the computer. Ethan rested against Emily, using her as a crutch.

Joe turned slightly as he worked and looked at Ethan with a grin. "Would you like to do the honors?"

Joe moved out of the way to reveal a strange keypad. There were multiple numbers and symbols. At the top, there was a single blue button with a glowing X.

"What do I do?"

"You just have to push that little blue button and watch the screen."

Ethan reached forward and pushed the button. Seconds after he jammed his finger onto the blue skull, camera two flashed a blinding brightness and then went dead.

Everyone stumbled back, rubbing their eyes in pain.

"What the hell was that," Emily protested.

Smiling like a proud papa, Joe patted the screen, "That was Old Glory."

Gerald looked at his friend, "You're kidding?"

"Nope. I was able to find one on the black market last year."

Sam butted in, "Can we be in on the joke? What's old glory?"

Joe turned to Sam, "Old Glory is the nickname for an explosive round used in anti-aircraft guns. The rounds have a volatile and highly unstable mix of explosives that have made the weapon obsolete in most military operations. You can only purchase these babies illegally."

"What exactly did it just do?"

"Let's just say that whoever the sniper was, he isn't anymore."

Emily shook her head, "Don't you think that's a little overkill?"

Ethan nudged her, "Hell no it wasn't! That was awesome."

Joe and Ethan shared an enthusiastic high-five causing Ethan to recoil in pain. It was here that Gerald interjected, "If we're done screwing around, can we please focus on the other men who are trying to kill us?"

Seconds after that last, poignant statement was spoken, the rear of the building exploded in flash of smoke and debris.

Chapter

Twelve

Sabre stood atop his perch, the RPG-7V still smoked in his hand. After he had seen Anton evaporate into a wall of flame, he had decided his side needed to become the aggressors. He had loaded one of the thermobaric rounds into his RPG, and unloaded onto the side of building three. Needless to say the weapon produced the desired effect; the entire south side of building three now lay in ruin. The explosion had been so intense its shockwave almost knocked him from his position.

Immediately after the explosion, Sabre called for his men to open fire on the complex. Holger and Amun drove their vehicle up to the side of building one and began to tear into it with the 50cal. The rounds tore through the siding like it was paper. Each round had the potential to travel the length of the complex with deadly accuracy, and from their position it was ideal for them to remain safe against any unexpected retaliation.

On cue, Franc and Tau also targeted the smoking building with their weapons. The roar of gunfire was deafening. Sabre knew that the explosion would soon draw the attention of the local authorities, so this needed to conclude as soon as possible.

$$\text{S}$$

The smoke had begun to clear as Sam regained consciousness. He was covered in soot and rock, and to his horror, he heard nothing save for a loud ringing in his ears. As he looked around at the devastation, he could see Joe and Gerald rushing about, each man now wildly firing large weapons he thought might be AK-47s.

Sam began to sit up when he realized that his legs were stuck under a sheet of metal from the roof. The sheet had crushed his right ankle and broke at least one bone in his left leg. Now that his mind was beginning to clear, the pain of his injuries overwhelmed him as he let out a scream of pure agony.

The shout drew the attention of Emily who was lost in the cloud of smoke. Emerging from the veil of debris, she flopped down next to him and began to shout for help. Sam just looked at her mouth as she screamed, hearing nothing but the awful ringing.

"EMILY," he shrieked. She shook him and began to speak a mile a minute. "I can't hear," he shouted. Pointing to his legs, Sam yelled, "Help me lift the metal."

She shook her head in acknowledgment and grabbed the side of the metal. She raised three fingers and shook them at him.

"Count of three," Sam howled back, understanding her intent.

Emily lowered one, then two, and finally the third finger. With as much strength as they could muster, the two lifted the metal with all of their might. At first it didn't budge, but after a second it began to shift. As Emily strained, the metal shifted enough for Sam to slide himself out from under his prison.

As soon as he was free, a second explosion tore through the building. Emily dropped the metal sheet and rushed to Sam's side. Grabbing him under the arms, she dragged him behind the now bullet ridden shell of the taxi cab.

Sam continued to howl in agony. His twisted legs were now covered in blood and dirt.

Moments later, Ethan appeared out of the dark, his wounded shoulder now seeping blood. "What happened?"

Emily pointed to the large metal sheet, "A piece of the ceiling collapsed on Sam's legs. I think he's hurt real bad."

Ethan looked at Sam's injuries and took quick stock of the situation. "I'll be right back," he shouted as he turned and fled back towards the door, remaining low as bullets continued to fly over his head.

Emily looked on in disbelief as Ethan disappeared around the side of the cab. Panicked, she pleaded for Ethan to stay, "Don't leave us!"

Now alone again, she covered Sam as the building was being destroyed all around them.

To her relief, only a few seconds passed before Ethan reappeared with Joe. The men crouched next to Sam and Joe gave his wounds a quick scan. He had the red bag with him and after surveying the scene, he began to rummage through it. Removing a large syringe and a vial of morphine, he filled the syringe with fluid and jammed the needle into Sam's arm. It only took a moment for the liquid to do its work. The shaking and screaming stopped and

Sam's body went limp. Joe checked Sam's pulse and looked up at the others.

Pointing to a door five feet behind them, Joe barked at the group, "He's stable. We need to move him into the bathroom."

Emily grabbed Joe's arm and shouted so he could hear her, "But what if the building collapses?"

"It won't matter, either way we're all dead. He has a better shot if we lay him in the tub. It's cast iron and can withstand a lot of abuse."

Emily reluctantly agreed with Joe's logic and helped the two men carry Sam's now lifeless body into the bathroom.

As they shut the door, Gerald rushed over to them. His right eye was covered with a patch and some gauze; a deep scratch peeked out from beneath the bandage. He held his AK-47 close to his chest, the barrel glowed red from the strain of the firefight. Breathing heavily, he pointed towards the now gaping hole in the wall, "There is…*pant*…someone on the south wall with a grenade launcher and two men in the…*pant*… north tree line with machine guns. The 50cal rounds are coming from the west. I don't know how many are there."

Joe slapped the brick wall, "When I rebuilt this place I reinforced the walls with steel, so baring any further rocket attacks, it should hold for a few more minutes."

Ethan ducked as a bullet ricocheted off of the wall above his head. "Screw that, we can't hold out much longer. We need a plan."

Joe crouched and ran over to the cab. He smacked the trunk and it sprung open. Inside was every weapon you could imagine; Ak-47s, Mac-10s, old Thompson sub-machine guns, M249 Saw machine guns, 50 cal Desert Eagles and more advanced weaponry that Gerald didn't even recognize.

Grinning with pride over his collection, Joe began to distribute the armaments. "Grab as much as you can carry," Joe commanded as he pulled an M-16 and multiple grenades out of the trunk. "It's time we said hi to our guests."

It had been eight minutes since the initial attack and Sabre was growing impatient. The structures surrounding building three were destroyed, but building three was annoyingly resilient. He had to wonder if it was reinforced with something. Lowering the RPG, he picked up his radio and called to his men. "Cease fire," he shouted into the mouthpiece.

All at once, the deafening sound of their weapons had stopped. Raising his binoculars, Sabre surveyed the damage, looking for any sign of life. "Holger is there any movement on your end?"

"*No sir.*"

"Tau do you have eyes on any survivors?"

"*That's a negative sir. We haven't seen anything since we began firing. There was some small arms fire but nothing of consequence.*"

After giving the compound one last look, Sabre put down the binoculars and keyed the radio again, "Tau, I want you and Franc to move in. Keep low and stand ready for anything."

"*Yes sir. We are already en route.*"

Sabre looked over to the entrance, "Holger, I want you and Amun to pull the truck around the rear of the building and use the winch to clear off some of this debris."

"*We are on the way sir.*"

Sabre remained perched on his tower as he watched his men close in for the kill. His pulse began to race as he realized how close they were to finally securing that which so many have had attempted to obtain but failed.

Holger had slowly angled his truck around the corner of what was left of building one. As he drove past the rubble of the other buildings he noticed Tau and Franc creeping ever closer to the entrance of the building, their weapons at the ready as they scanned for survivors. He had worked with these men for many years now, and he felt privileged to have been a part of such a proficient team of soldiers.

Slowly he pulled the vehicle directly in front of the massive hole that Sabre created with his toy. Amun kept the barrel of the massive machine gun pointed into the opening as the truck inched to a halt.

As Holger began to climb out of the vehicle, a grenade emerged from the dust and crashed through the window of the Humvee. Amun shouted in despair as the truck erupted into a ball of fire. Holger was catapulted through the air and he landed twenty feet away, motionless; his large form now a ball of scorched flesh.

Sabre looked on in shock as pieces of Amun continued to land over a large area. As he prepared to launch another rocket at the building, the silo was lit up with heavy machine gun fire, forcing him to jump off the back of the tower. The thirty-five foot drop dazed him for a moment, but he was mostly unharmed. The soil around his position erupted with dust from the relentless barrage of bullets. "I need cover fire, ASAP," he shouted into his radio.

As Tau and Franc sprinted around the corner of building three, a spray of ammunition forced them to retreat back behind the building. Gerald and Joe had emerged from the structure with machine guns in both hands. The grizzled veterans fired at the targets with lethal accuracy.

Ethan and Emily both followed with Sam dangling limp between them. The plan was to make it to an old pick-up truck Joe had in the garage just south of where they were.

As the old friends laid down cover fire, Ethan and Emily made a break for the small building. They were slowed greatly by Sam's dead weight and Ethan's injured shoulder, but they pressed on as fast as they could. Sabre continued to cower behind the silo, waiting for the right moment to strike.

Franc and Tau were now returning fire the best they could. Joe and Gerald held the better position and had excellent cover within the ruins of the building.

During his leap, Sabre lost his RPG and was left with nothing but one hand grenade and his trusty SIG SP 2022 that never left his hip. He pulled the weapon from its holster and prepared for what may have been his final stand. As he began to turn towards the oncoming fire, Sabre noticed the three fugitives limping towards a small building not three hundred feet from his location.

At that distance it was hard to make out who they were, but it appeared to be the children and another man, maybe the sheriff. As he quickly surveyed the group, Sabre noticed that all three had backpacks with them. He couldn't be certain, but if one of these bags had the map in it he needed to stop them from escaping.

He reached into his jacket pocket and pulled out a small green orb. He stood from his position and flattened his body against the silo to avoid the relentless attack. After calming his breathing, he marked off the distance in his head. He pulled the pin on top of the grenade, and with all of his strength, heaved the small explosive towards its target.

ᔑ

Due to their injuries, Joe had decided that Ethan and Sam needed to escape the ambush as soon as possible. As he helped them load the rest of the gear, Joe remembered the small pick-up truck that was parked in a garage on the southern part of the property. If Ethan and the kids could make it to the vehicle, they just might make it out alive.

It was his intent to have Gerald help him in creating a distraction while Emily and Ethan carried Sam to the vehicle. Ethan put up a fight over the plan, but his protest fell on deaf ears. Joe had made up his mind and that was that.

Gerald, Emily and Ethan had recovered Sam from the bathtub and staged him near the side door to the complex. Lucky for them, the explosion didn't damage or block the door. Gerald had decided to keep the lockbox with Sam for the time being, just in case he didn't make it out of the ensuing attack.

Gerald pulled Ethan aside before beginning his assault, "I need you make sure the kids make it out safe. I know that my actions have caused all of you terrible pain and I only hope my sacrifice will give all of you a chance at a new life."

Ethan shifted his pack off of his bad shoulder, "We all lost something and there isn't anything that will make it better, but I will do my best to make things right by you. It just might take some time."

"I do have one last request of you, Ethan."

"You want me to take care of that damn box, don't ya?"

"I do. With me and Joe out of the picture, there is no one else I trust this secret with. It's up to you and the kids to keep this treasure a secret from the world."

"Why don't you just burn the damn thing? Then nobody will ever know where it was."

Gerald grabbed Ethan by the shoulder straps and pulled him closer, causing Ethan to grimace. "That map must not be damaged. If the location was ever discovered, the destruction that would be unleashed is too terrible to fathom. Part of your responsibility is to remain vigilant in keeping an eye on the area surrounding the meteors location. If it seems like it is in danger of being discovered, you may have to move it."

Ethan pulled away from Gerald's grasp, "How the hell do I move something like that without anyone knowing?"

Gerald removed a small notebook from his pack and handed it to Ethan. "This book includes the code to the box and account numbers to multiple bank accounts around the world. There are also addresses to safe houses all over Europe and Asia, which Joe and I used back in the day. You now have the assets needed to make almost anything happen if you chose," Gerald turned and pointed towards Sam and Emily, "and you have the best support system you could have ever asked for."

Ethan held the small notebook in his hands and thought about the weight of his new responsibilities. Not only was he now the guardian of two emotionally damaged teenagers, he also held the key to one of the most destructive substances on the planet. "I guess I really don't have much of a choice do I?"

Gerald smiled and slapped Ethan on his good shoulder, "That's the spirit young fella. Now let's get this show on the road."

As Gerald joined Joe by the large hole in the wall, Ethan rejoined Sam and Emily.

"What did he want," Emily asked after curiously watching the entire exchange.

"I really don't want to talk about it. Are you ready to do this?"

Emily winked at her big brother, "As ready as I'll ever be."

Together they lifted Sam to his feet and each took an arm in support of the boy. His size and weight were a challenge for them to handle, but the adrenaline now flowing through their veins helped give them the strength they needed. Once they had him secured in place, Ethan slid the little notebook into Sam's bag. He wanted all the eggs in one basket.

As if on cue, there was a lull in the action outside, so the group used this as a sign to make their move. Gerald and Joe had armed themselves with multiple grenades and rifles, each man prepared to give their lives for the safety of the children.

Joe extended his hand to Gerald, "Are you ready old friend?"

"It's been an honor to serve alongside of you Joe," Gerald said as he accepted the gesture with his own hand.

After a second of silent reassurance, the two men released hands and prepared for battle.

Joe carefully removed a grenade from his belt and pulled the pin. He turned to Ethan, "As soon as the firing starts, wait a few and then make a break for it. Understood?"

"Good luck old man. See ya at the truck," Ethan said with remorse in his voice. He knew this was quite possibly the end, and he regretted not being able to take a few of the bastards with him.

Joe took a deep breath and let the lever go. He threw the ball of death into the sun-lit cloud of dust and debris.

The sound of glass breaking was followed by a shriek of terror and a large explosion. Gerald was the first to advance after the blast, his Thompson machine gun roaring a welcome to the intruders. Joe was hot on his heels, his weapon singing in tune with Gerald's.

Ethan and Emily couldn't help but be in awe of the two men. "Let's go," Ethan shouted as enough time had passed for them to sneak out under the cover of fire.

After passing through the door, they were able to clear the building and maneuver around what was left of one of the attackers. A single boot smoldered in the dirt, the foot and lower leg of its owner still inside.

They were pushing themselves as much as their legs could take. As the battle raged behind them, Ethan was the first to see the small building Joe had mentioned and he began to pick up the pace.

"We're almost there Sam," Emily said as much reassuring herself as she was her brother. The sound of gunfire was beginning to fade into the distance as they inched closer to their target.

Ethan was focused forward, but as they neared the building he turned his attention back to the fire fight. It was then that he saw a man in the distance heave a small object in their direction. He didn't need any help understanding what was headed their way.

Without saying a word, he shoved Sam and Emily as hard as he could. Both kids rolled off to the side in shock, as they were unprepared for the sudden move. As the grenade fell at his feet, Ethan did the only thing he could to save the kids. With a sudden flop, Ethan collapsed onto the device as it exploded.

The force of the blast sent Emily flailing through the air and into a tree, knocking her unconscious. Sam was propelled back into a pile of rocks. His limp form was smoldering from the violent explosion.

Joe and Gerald had been occupied with the two men hiding around the corner of the building when the explosion shook them to their core. Joe was the first to turn and see the horrific scene. Emily and Sam both lay motionless, he scanned for Ethan but there was no trace of him anywhere.

"Cover me," he yelled to his partner.

With Gerald laying down a deadly barrage, Joe sprinted towards the children. As he drew closer to the scene, Joe surveyed the area for the cause of the blast. Just past the silo he saw a man in black running towards the train tracks. He considered pursuing the man, but changed his mind when he heard a moan emanate from Emily.

Rushing to her side, he was grateful to find her semiconscious, but otherwise unharmed.
Joe grabbed her arm and pulled her up slowly, "Emily, can you move?"

She rubbed her throbbing head and tried to focus on the situation, "Uhh… Where's Sam?"

Joe looked over to Sam, who lay motionless on the ground.

"He's over there," Joe said as he pointed to Sam, "You stay here, I'll check on him."

Joe sat Emily against the tree she had collided with, and began to run towards Sam. After he took his first two steps, he happened to look over at the last spot he saw the man in black. To his shock, the man now was kneeling; a rocket launch perched on his shoulder facing their position. "Duck," he shouted as he turned and dove on top of Emily.

There was a brief whizzing sound as the grenade flew over their heads. It exploded between them and Sam, causing a tidal wave of dirt and fire to pour over them.

ᶠ

Gerald had continued to keep the others occupied when he felt the shockwave of the explosion. He chanced a quick glance at the source of the blast, not sure of what he would find. To his dismay the remainder of the group was hidden by smoke and earth. Fearing the worst, Gerald let out a primal scream and charged the attackers still taking cover behind the wall. His sudden aggressive movement surprised them, causing both men to lose focus.

Gerald dove for the corner of building three, his Thompson peppering the targets with deadly accuracy. He felt the same adrenaline rush he had felt on that cold night fifty years earlier. Franc and Tau never stood a chance. Their bodies shook with each connection, both men taking multiple hits before they finally succumbed to their injuries.

Regardless of the fact that they had both been neutralized, Gerald continued to unload on their lifeless bodies, his rage flowing through his trigger finger. He continued until the weapon just clicked, his magazine having long since expiring.

Collecting himself, Gerald looked back towards the site of the blast. From this distance he was still unsure if anyone was alive, but he did see something that caused him alarm. Not two-hundred yards from their location a man in black was methodically walking towards the fiery scene.

Chapter
Thirteen

December 25th, 1963
Toulon, France

It was Christmas morning and the holiday spirit had taken hold of the Mediterranean town of Toulon. The local children ran through the streets, singing songs and playing with the new treasure found under their trees earlier that morning, while the adults began preparing the holiday feasts that made the salty sea air smell like heaven on earth. The entire town bustled with cheers of joy and love, except for one family; tucked away near the coast stood a small seaside villa belonging to the Douay family.

Maslin and Brie Douay had lived in Toulon their entire lives. They had met in grade school and a lifelong romance had blossomed after years of playful flirtation.

Maslin was a gifted individual in many ways, and his abilities with firearms would eventually lead him into a life as a Marksman in the French Navy during World War II. Upon his safe return from his final post in Berlin, it wasn't long before this decorated soldier would attract the attention of interested parties, one being an organization that used men of his skill set to cause anarchy around the globe.

At first he wasn't sure of the tactics used by his new employers, but he couldn't argue with the money. In one day he would make as much as he did in a month working the docks near his home. He also found a satisfaction in causing pain to those he deemed evil. This was an unexpected side effect of his work, but also one that made him a more proficient weapon.

As his status grew within the organization, his home life was taking a toll, due to the responsibilities that kept him away, and his inability to be truthful with Brie over what he actually did with the company. After an unusually long mission in Russia, he returned home and vowed to Brie that their marriage would be the top priority. His employers had decided to be generous with Maslin due to his contributions to the cause, granting him an extended leave from field work.

Two weeks into his return, a miracle happened. After years of trying and many failed attempts, Brie became pregnant with their first child.

On February 13, 1961, a little boy they named Ciel Douay was born. This child was perfect in every way. At the moment of his birth he didn't even cry; as the doctor pulled him from his mother's womb, Ciel just looked around at the world with a wide eyed curiosity.

Two years after his son's birth, Maslin was approached with a delicate mission in America, and it was insinuated that declining wasn't an option.

It was early October when he received his orders and he spent his last day at home playing with Ciel. He hadn't left the young boys side for more than a day since his birth, and the thought of being away for any length of time tortured him.

The day of the trip, Maslin kissed his wife and young son goodbye then boarded a plane for America with two of his best men. That was the last time Brie and Ciel would see him alive.

Over the next month, Brie received daily calls from Maslin. Each conversation was filled with stories of his trip and she regaled him with tales of the daily adventures she was having with young Ciel. In late November, the calls suddenly stopped.

Then on Christmas Eve, Brie received a call from Cinjon Ames, one of Maslin's friends in the organization. When the phone rang she knew that something had happened, but the news still devastated her. She was told that Maslin was assaulted while dealing with a dangerous fugitive and he was murdered during the struggle.

In her despondent state, she placed Ciel in his crib that evening and then walked into the ocean. Three days had passed before anyone noticed that she was gone, her suicide going unnoticed due to her body being washed out to sea.

It was Cinjon who decided to check in on Brie after not being able to reach her for a few days. Upon his arrival he was stunned to find Ciel alone in the dark home he shared with his parents. Other than the boy, it was obvious that no one else had been there for quite some time.

Cinjon collected the hungry child and brought him to the organization's elders. It was decided that he would be taken care of by the group, in honor of Maslin's sacrifice. Cinjon volunteered to mentor the boy as if he was his own.

Over the next twenty years, Ciel was instructed by the greatest minds in Europe. He excelled in all forms of study, becoming fluent in multiple languages by the time he was sixteen. His combat lessons were as intense as anything he learned in the classroom.

After basic military training, Ciel was taught multiple forms of martial arts as well as firearms and military strategy. It was after his eighteenth birthday that Cinjon revealed to Ciel the truth behind his parents' deaths.

As expected, he didn't take the news well. A rage began to grow within him from that moment on, and it was about to be unleashed onto the world.

Ciel completed his training earlier than expected and he was immediately activated as an agent. It was during his first year in the field that he had decided to take his father's middle name as his own and Sabre was born.

The next two decades were filled with great success for the young agent. He had gained a reputation as not only a cunning intellectual, but also as an unstable psychopath.

His main allegiance was to the organization, but he always kept his hope alive that one day he would find the man that took his family from him.

$\backslash\int$

Joliet, Illinois
Present day

Sabre brushed the dirt off of his suit as he walked towards the charred ruins he had just created. His long journey was coming to an end and it filled him with a peace he hadn't felt for some time. As he approached Joe's motionless body, a bullet grazed his cheek. Turning abruptly, he was not prepared for who he saw pointing a gun at him.

Gerald had his 9mm pointed at Sabre; the last round he fired emptied the smoking firearm. Exhausted from the battle, Gerald unconsciously kept pulling the trigger on the gun. With each click of the fire pin hitting nothing, it was clear to his opponent that he was helpless.

Sabre stared at the old man with disbelief, "It's you?"

Gerald threw his weapon to the ground and pulled a knife from his belt, "Let's go you son of a bitch. Fight me like a man."

Sabre studied his opponent, "I can't believe it's really you."

Growing frustrated by the inane back and forth, Gerald spit on the ground at Sabre's feet, "I don't know who you think I am, but I would remember a piece of garbage like you."

"You are correct, we haven't met; but you do know my father, intimately."

Gerald eased up his posturing and squinted in the sun to get a better look at Sabre, "Who are you?"

"My name is Ciel Douay, and you changed my life fifty years ago on a cold night in Oregon. That's the night you killed my father."

Gerald froze in his place as he relieved that terrible night in his mind. He didn't get a good look at the men he killed that day, but he would never forget the accent of the interrogator, the French accent. His limbs went numb as he realized that his past demons had finally come back to exact their vengeance upon him.

Sabre raised his firearm and began to unload into Gerald's chest; each round carried with it the furry of a child's loss. As Sabre pulled the trigger, years of anger and pain over the loss of his parents melted away in a frenzy of emotion. He began to cry as the sound of his maniacal laughter began to drown out the explosion of each round leaving his gun.

Gerald's body was propelled through the air and onto the charred earth behind him. As it hit the ground, Sabre continued to pull the trigger until the last round was fired. The world around him didn't exist at this moment; it was just him and glorious vengeance. Today was the greatest day of his life.

Emily awoke with Sabre's first shot, surprised to find Joe's unconscious body sprawled out on top of hers. She knew that he had probably saved her life, but she was unsure if he was alive or dead.

She was able to move him enough to get a look around. It was then that she saw the man in black unloading his weapon on Gerald with a feverish intensity. Fearing for the life of her brother who lay not two feet from where Gerald was being brutally executed, Emily fought even harder to move the large man off of her. She struggled with everything she had, but to no avail.

Her body was bruised and battered, her family and friends were all dead, and there was no way that Sam or Gerald could have survived the brutal attack she had just witnessed. Emily had almost given up hope, when she heard the man's weapon finally click after the last round was spent; that's when she saw it. Protruding from Joe's coat was the handle of a pistol.

With one last desperate heave, Emily moved Joe enough to free up her arm and grab the pistol. As she pulled it free, the man had turned towards her as he reloaded his weapon. Realizing what she was doing, he became alarmed and raised his gun to fire, but it was too late. Emily squeezed the trigger and unloaded the full magazine into the man's chest.

Sabre's body shook with subtle tremors as the rounds ripped through his chest. He hit the turf with a large thud and became still after a few more convulsions. Emily continued to point the weapon at what was left of their attacker, her hand clenched around the pistol grip.

As her breathing became faster due to shock, she began to hyperventilate. Her head started to pound, the world spun around her and she slipped into unconsciousness.

Chapter
Fourteen

The turbulence snapped Emily out of her dream, her hand clenched as if still holding the pistol that ended the life of another. Her memory of shooting the man in black replayed over in her head. His chest exploding into a sea of red had become the screensaver of her subconscious.

She wiped the sleep from her eyes as she tried to adjust to her new surroundings. Soft music and air conditioning had replaced the smoke and gunfire of the battle. She was sprawled out over two seats of a plane of some kind. Her clothes had been changed and an IV pumped some kind of clear fluid into her veins. She sat up and looked around the cabin. It wasn't a large plane; in fact she recognized the interior from the last flight she had taken. This was the same Cessna that brought Sam and her to Chicago.

The sky outside was dark, the only light coming from the brilliant moon looking in the window at her. She sat up and disconnected the IV from her arm. As she stood, the world once again spun, forcing her back down into her seat.

"Careful," a voice echoed from the cockpit. "You've been out for two days."

She looked up at the familiar voice. "Where are we?"

Joe entered the cabin and sat down next to her. His face was covered in bruises and there was a line of stitches across his left cheek. As he approached her seat, she noticed he had acquired a slight limp that looked to cause him pain with each step.

"We are twenty-thousand feet in the air on our way to Scotland."

"Scotland? Why are we going there? What happened?" Her head beginning to clear, she finally realized that something was missing and sprang to her feet. "Where's Sam?"

The sudden movement caused her to once again pitch forward and clutch the seat.

"Careful now Emily, just sit down. I think you might have a concussion and you need to relax. It's actually a miracle you're alive."

She sat back into her seat and looked into Joe's eyes, "Where is my brother?"

"How much do you remember about that day?"

Emily closed her eyes and once again stared into the face of the man in black as he was flung back from the force of her attack.

"I remember helping Ethan carry Sam towards the garage. We were so close when I was suddenly shoved back. A second latter I was flying through the air then nothing." As the sad realization of their other missing comrade hit her, Emily grabbed Joe's wrist, "Ethan. Joe what happened to Ethan?"

Joe's solemn expression answered her question before he even spoke a word. "Ethan didn't make it. I didn't see it happen, but after what you just told me I can assume he sacrificed himself to save you and Sam. I'm truly sorry. He was a great man."

Emily turned her attention back to the night sky outside of her window. She didn't shed a tear over the news, even though she knew she should. Her sadness and pain had reached a level that made her numb.

Trying to get her focused back on the situation at hand, Joe shook her leg, "Hey kiddo. I need you to refocus on what happened after the explosion."

Emily turned her expressionless face towards Joe, "When I awoke, you were hunched over me and I thought you might be dead. It was then that I saw the man in black. He had a gun in his hand and he was shooting Mr. Kerr over and over. He had caused us so much pain that I knew something had to be done to finally stop him, so I grabbed your gun and shot him." This last statement caused her to rub her head. "I see him in my sleep. His body is just a mess of blood. I can't stop thinking about it."

Joe put his hand on her knee, "You did what you had to do. I hope you know that we are both here because of your bravery. Thank you for that."

"Who was he?"

"After doing some checking, I was able to match him with an operative working for ECHO. He had many aliases, but the name that continued to pop up was Sabre. I believe he was the man behind the attack on your town."

Emily closed her eyes, preparing for what was to come next. "Where is my brother?"

Joe picked up a water bottle and took a long swig before continuing, "I awoke just as the sound of police sirens could be heard in the distance. Sabre was dead and Gerald was gone along with your brother. I was hoping you might have seen something.

Emily opened her eyes, "How? I saw Mr. Kerr shot a million times. He was dead. How could he have gotten up and walked away after being shot a thousand times?"

Joe smiled, "I can't answer that. What I do know is that he is one stubborn old fool with a big bag of tricks. He's not dying 'til he's good and ready."

Emily pitched forward and slapped the armrest, her new found ferocity erupting into a suppressed rage, "How could we just leave without knowing what happened to them?"

Joe raised his hands in hopes of calming her, "Calm down. Gerald must have grabbed Sam before he left. I can only assume that he thought we were dead, and in the confusion of the situation just helped the one person he thought he could. I'm sorry Emily, but we needed to get out of there, and I'm sure Sam would have wanted you to be safe."

"What about the lockbox? Please tell me the reason for this entire mess didn't fall into ECHO's hands."

"The box was in Sam's backpack so I can only guess that it's with him and Gerald wherever they are. Hell, it could have been destroyed in the attack. I'm afraid once again that I just don't know."

The news was like a dull knife in her side. She sat back, shifting her gaze out her window. "What now," she mumbled as her focus once again centered around the brilliant light that filled the night sky.

"We need to disappear. I have a small place in Glasgow that we can hole up in." He reached for her hand in a weak gesture of condolence. To his shock, her hand was warm, but also lifeless; the events of the past week causing more damage to her soul than her physical self.

She remained motionless as her hollow gaze remained focused out the small window.
Joe let go of her hand and moved back into the cockpit. He had seen many things during his years in the CIA, but he still wasn't ready for the pain he felt for this young woman.

Two weeks ago, Emily Lana had been just another American teenager trying to make her way in the world. She had a family that loved her and a bright future. Today she is an empty shell, with only her nightmares to comfort her.

Her world had crumbled around her, but there was another one on the other side of the darkness.

Epilogue

June 6th, 2015
Palermo, Sicily

A warm summer breeze roused the small group of seagulls that perched just below the second floor balcony of the rundown eighteenth century villa. This dilapidated home was situated in a prime location just off the coast of the Mediterranean, and it was the home to many creatures big and small.

As the birds flew off into the night sky, the petite form of a young woman in a flowing summer dress emerged from the structure to watch their flight.

Her posture was that of a confident woman twice her age, each curve rippled with the lean muscle of an athlete.

The long black hair that once flowed over her shoulders like the gentle trickle of a brook in the twilight, was now replaced by a blonde pixy cut, slightly curled in the front. The now exposed skin of her neck caused her to shiver with every gentle breeze.

She had called this place home for the past three months, but she never tired of the view.

As she took in the scenery, a man walked up from behind and put his hand on her shoulder.

As she reached over and patted his hand, she shook her head in disgust, "You know I heard you before you even climbed the stairs. You're getting sloppy in your old age."

The man pulled his hand away as he sat down on one of the chairs that adorned the balcony, "Now listen here young lady, I might not be as flexible as I used to be, but I can still whoop your butt in a fight."

Emily just smirked at his posturing, "Dream on, Joe. I'm eighty years younger than you and besides, you taught me too well." She kicked his chair before taking the seat across from her aging mentor.

Shifting his attention away from the abusive teen, Joe looked out over the water as if he was in heaven, "Beautiful isn't it. I haven't been here in well over a decade, but I will always call this place home."

"I still can't believe your family owns this place. It could use a fresh coat of paint and an exterminator's touch, but all in all, it's not too shabby."

The two friends spent the next few minutes in quiet reflection. It had been two years since the tragedy in Shashone Peak, and they had been on the move ever since. Once Joe landed their plane in Scotland, he had spent a few months searching the many resources he still had for any sign that either Gerald or Sam was still alive.

During this time he had spent multiple hours each day instructing Emily in everything he knew about survival and combat. If she was to become his ward, then she better know how to handle herself in a fight.

Gerald's trail never heated up, it looked as if his old friend still had a few tricks up his sleeve; Joe just hoped that once the dust had settled, Gerald would find them.

There was increasing chatter pertaining to Joe and his group. ECHO seemed desperate to find the one's responsible for the death of one of its best agents, and they never gave up their pursuit of the lockbox. This constant danger forced Joe and Emily to move around as much as possible.

One month they would be in The Netherlands, then the next six they would spend in Budapest. The one constant that always remained the same was Emily's training. At first Joe had trained her as a way to protect her, but now she had advanced enough to become a viable and willing partner in Joe's endgame to wipe every trace of ECHO off of the face of the earth.

The time had to be closing in on 9:30pm when the doorbell rang. Emily was about to get up when Joe motioned for her to stay. "I'm not expecting any visitors. Get in position and wait for my signal."

As Joe got up from his seat, he removed a GLOCK 19 from his ankle holster. Emily reached under her chair and removed the compact 9mm Beretta Storm Joe got her for her birthday this past year. It was one of her favorite possessions and she had become very proficient with it.

After checking her magazine, she leapt over the edge of the balcony, catching the drain pipe that ran down the side. She had used this method almost every night to sneak out to the local bars after Joe went to bed.

Joe made his way to the front door while Emily shimmied down the drainpipe leading to the first floor.

After reaching the ground, she silently made her way to the front, keeping herself hidden behind the tall bushes that decorated the front of the Villa.

As she peered around the corner, she could see the back of a man's head. He was tall, at least six foot or more.

She couldn't see his face due to the Yankee cap that covered most of his blonde hair. His baggy Hawaiian shirt and cargo shorts hung loosely from his skinny frame.

He couldn't have weighed more than a buck sixty, tops. His legs and arms were covered with multiple tattoos which seemed to hide some serious scars. But none of this mattered because whoever he was, he picked the wrong damn house.

Emily was focused on the stranger as Joe opened the door.

Joe smiled and acknowledged their guest, "Can I help yo…"

It took Emily a second to notice the look of shock on Joe's face as his words of greeting fell short.

The stranger broke the silence first, "I finally found you?"

Emily slowly lowered her weapon. It had been an eternity, but she knew that voice. It was the same voice that used to torment her when she would take too long in the bathroom.

The same voice that consoled her when her parents were murdered.

Stepping from the shadows she approached the man's back, "Sam? How did you...?"

Samuel Lana turned towards his baby sister, a silver box in his heavily scarred hands.

"I'm Superman, remember?"

The End?

Here is a glimpse at the next exciting chapter in the Lockbox series

ECHO

Coming 2016

Prologue

June 3, 1348
Ferrara, Italy

Throughout the bustling streets of Ferrara, the corpses of those who had succumbed to the mysterious illness from the west, were piled like refuse waiting to be collected. The rancid aroma of rotting flesh was overpowering.

The terror of this malady was everlasting. Once you had become accustomed to the smell of the dead, you would then have to deal with the moans and wailing of the dying and those who mourned them.

This small Italian town had originally been isolated from the disease, but after the pestilence was brought to

Genoa, it soon spread over Europe like a wild fire out of control.

The early warning signs soon became apparent. First you heard the coughing, followed by a small outbreak of fever. After a while the black, oozing boils would appear, proceeded by the enviable demise of the infirmed.

Most of the civilians knew little of this plague, their only information and comfort coming from the church and its insistence on faith in these trying times.

A mile out of the city, Ciro del Pino and his family owned a small goat farm surrounded by the most beautiful landscape imaginable.

The trees flowered each spring with pink and white petals that chased each other in the breeze like children playing tag. Just behind the home was a brook that flowed from the nearby hills. Its waters would attract the local wildlife, who gleefully bathed and romped in its cool waters.

After the outbreak, Ciro and his wife did everything to keep their family safe from the reach of the disease, but they had failed. Their young son Aldo had contracted the disease in May and by early June he was gone.

Now Ciro's wife Elena lay wrapped in blankets, shivering and crying as the agony from her ever crippling malady drove her mad with despair.

Seemingly immune to the effects of the disease, Ciro never fell victim to its touch, and each passing day he watched his lovely young wife slip evermore into its grasp.

Elena was all he had left in the world and she was quickly slipping away. Day in and day out he would remain steadfast by her side.

〜

It was on a dark and tempestuous summer's morning that a stranger would stagger in from the deluge. His crimson cloak billowed in the wind as a powerful gale forced open the door to the small farmhouse.

After slamming the door behind him, the large man removed his cloak and shook the water from his head. His ominous frame was covered with an immense tan doublet that was adorned with blood stains and char.

The giant's heavily scarred hands and face were a resume of one who has seen the glory of battle on many occasions.

He was grand in stature and each piece of his attire was worn and tattered save for the small trinket fastened to the left side of his collar. It appeared to be an onyx stone Greek E covering a P:

"For Christ sake," the man grumbled as he shook the water from his head. "What a bloody mess out there. It's as if the gods themselves are trying to wash us from the earth."

Surveying the small house, the man was perplexed by the lack of interest over his arrival. In the corner of the room, Ciro silently wept, Elena's cold hand in his. The frail woman now lay motionless, her deep brown eyes stared off into nothingness.

Realizing what had occurred, the large man removed the mighty broad sword from is hip and flung it to the ground with a mighty clang.

"Stop your wailing boy. You sound like a bloody woman"

Ciro wiped the tears from his eyes and turned to face the man. "Get the hell out of my home and leave me in peace."

The man roared with laughter at the feeble demands of the broken man before him, "Well it seems like you have some balls after all." Wiping the spit from the corners of his mouth, the man sat down at a small wooden table that stood adjacent to the hearth. "Now bring me some wine boy, I have traveled far."

"You must not have heard me," Ciro spoke behind his clenched teeth. "I would appreciate it if you left me and my wife alone." Ciro gently set down Elena's hand and reached for his sword as he stood on his quivering legs.

This caused the man to once again erupt in a fit of unbridles laughter. "Put that away before you do something stupid. You're just like your mother, too goddamn emotional."

Enraged by the jab, Ciro charged his father with his sword held high. As he approached, the much larger man pushed the table away with his powerful arms, striking Ciro in the midsection with the solid piece of timber.

Standing with a quickness of someone half his size, Ciro's father stuck the stunned man in the face with one mighty strike, sending him soaring across the room and into a pile of firewood stacked in the rear of the cabin.

"You must have a death wish boy. You dare you raise your sword to your own father?"

Crawling to his knees, Ciro wiped the blood from his nose. "I would gladly leave this fowl world in peace with the knowledge that you will be joining me in hell."

The towering figure lumbered over to Ciro and smacked him in the mouth with his massive right hand. "No son of Tano del Pino will speak him this way. You don't have to like me, but you will obey and respect me. You were not raised to be weak."

Tano grabbed the trembling arm of his son and dragged his semi-conscious body over to the table, dropping him on the bench with a resounding thud.

Ciro coughed up a handful of blood as he tried to sit up, "A weak man doesn't ask for death, he fears it. I neither fear nor run from death. I will welcome its embrace with open arms."

"Great, now you're a poet." Wiping the blood from his hands, Tano slammed his fist into the table.

"I have traveled a great distance to see you and I'm not leaving until we come to an understanding."

Ciro just chuckled at the thought of him and his father agreeing over anything. "What understanding is this?"

"You need to realize that you're my flesh and blood and when I need your help, you will do whatever you can to help me. And I need your assistance with something of the utmost importance."

This caused Ciro to spit a well of blood onto Tano's large hand. In one quick motion, Tano backhanded Ciro in the mouth, causing him to collapse onto the table. Fighting to remain conscious, he shook his head in hope that it would cause the room to stop spinning.

As Ciro was composing himself, Tano made his way into the pantry and retrieved a bottle of wine and two glasses. Sitting back across from Ciro, he poured two large glasses of wine and emptied his in one massive gulp.

"Are you finished with your belly aching?"

Ciro raised his head enough to look into his father's eyes, "I'm ready to listen, but if I'm finished will depend on what you say next old man."

"Fair enough, now drink something and listen. What I'm about to tell you will change your life and the hopefully the lives of everyone in all of the many kingdoms across the land."

ς

Tano had fought for many lords in his day, but it was his time fighting for the church that he truly found the meaning of hypocrisy.

For five years he was tasked with hunting down and slaughtering nonbelievers with whom his masters in Rome had issue with. Each life taken was done so in the name of the one true God.

It didn't matter age, color, or nationality. He was blinded by faith and the promise of redemption after all that he had done in his life.

The irony was that nothing he could have even dreamed of doing prior to his employment with the church could compare to striking down infants still suckling their mother's breast. Those visions still haunted him to this day.

The sadness and doubt that pushed him to the brink of insanity still couldn't sway his focus and allegiance. He would do his job and with each life he took, Tano had believed that his passage into the next world was secure.

Six months prior to entering Ciro's home, Tano would find himself at a crossroads. There was a small group of men like him who began to question the true intentions of the church and its leaders, but at first they were nothing more than whispers in the shadows. These whispers would soon become deafening.

Those who were in the deepest confidence of the church hierarchy had heard rumors of a dark plague. This malady had begun to spread across the land, striking down those who acquired it with a ferocity and speed not seen before.

Tano watched friends and lovers die in mere days after showing the first sign of symptoms. When he sought help, he was told to pray for the souls of the sick and that the love of the lord would protect them.

With each death, his faith would diminish. Now stricken with grief and the frustration of his many unanswered prayers, he would find himself seeking out the help of those he had once brutalized.

Science would soon become his new God. It would infuriate him to learn that this plague was something that could be prevented with the proper precautions, precautions that were downplayed by the church. Faith was soon replaced by logic and enlightenment, all fueled by rage over what he had lost.

Tano would soon gather together a small group of men from his inner circle. These soldiers had spilled the same blood that he had, and now he was going to partner with them in a crusade of vengeance against the most power organization in the world, little did he know that this crusade would give birth to so much more.

Before he could begin, all Tano needed was the one piece he knew could bring the whole puzzle into focus. His son.

ᔑ

Ciro sat back and contemplated all he had just heard.

"I don't understand why you would need my help? We've barely spoken in the last ten years."

"You are not just my son, but also one of the best fighters I have even gone to battle with. Or at least you used to be."

Tano raised his glass and downed another gulp of wine, "What you have become is shameful. You used to be the best, a man worthy of my name and lineage. But now you look as weak as that rotting corpse."

Tano points over to the candle lit bed in the back.

This enrages Ciro who slapped the cup from his father's hand and swiftly buried the tip of a small dagger into Tano's throat.

"Don't you ever speak of her in that way again or I will cut your throat."

Tano shook his head in approval, "Now, that's the man I once knew. If it would help things move along, then I do apologize for my lack of respect, but I am not sorry for helping you remember what you are, and that's a killer."

Tano slowly pulled the blade from his throat as Ciro's hands shook with rage.

"Now the question is, what will you do with this information? Will you wallow in misery with the ghosts of those you lost, or will you join me and enact vengeance against those who helped cause your pain?"

৲

Ciro looked over to the peaceful remains of his beloved Elena, lying motionless in the dark, then back to the insignia in his hand.

Following a brief moment of silent reflection, he arose from his seat. In the corner of the room there was a rotting, wooden chest. Ciro made his way over to it and broke the seal that had kept its contents hidden from his family. Within in the chest was the tool of a violent life from a time long ago.

After dressing in a mix of armor and musty clothing, he retrieved his sword from the floor and attached it to his hip. Kneeling next to his wife's bed, he said his goodbyes.

"I'm sorry that I was not able to help you my love. You and Aldo will always be in my thoughts, and I only ask that you both hide your eyes from what I am about to do. I want you to remember me as the man you knew, not the man I truly am."

He leaned in and kissed her cold skin. As Ciro stood he grabbed the large blanket that covered his wife's lifeless form. Inhaling the sweet smell of death that enveloped the soft fabric, he would exhale his last breath as a loving husband and father, and become someone, something else. As he reached for the door, Ciro tossed the blanket onto the candles that surrounded his love.

Tano looked on impatiently as Ciro exited the house. The tempest that had raged for the last few days, still punished the countryside with its awesome force. Rain fell sideways across the nearby fields, but nothing seemed to faze the two men or their steeds.

Ciro mounted his horse and took one last look at the home that he had sacrificed so much for.

"I'm ready."

Tano nodded his approval and slowly led them into the darkness. As the two men disappeared into the night, the small structure burst into flames, the bleak howling of the relentless storm was now illuminated by the glow of the inferno.

The devil had called upon the small farm house tonight, and with him the fires of hell were about to be unleashed upon the world.

TO BE CONTINUED